AUTHOR & ILLUSTRATOR:
M. Villaire

—deepest regards to all who helped in this manuscript

Published by:
Bunny Village Press
Kalamazoo, MI USA

First publication 2025

You & i

intro

You changes.

But the li remains the same.

Oh yeah, lowercase or uppercase as if it matters—like it's the difference in standing between fresh-men or seniors, or something evolutionary. I really don't see it as different, anymore, the chip. In freshman year (should that be capitalized?) I toyed with an idea for a philosophical blab book that contemplated differences between the (little) i and the I.

Of course it was brilliant shit. That's the way it is with things in the mind's eye. We see a thing as already polished. That diamond in the rough never got hewn, though. It was about the disconnect, or I mean, it was to be about the disconnect. I held possessively to the title, because a good title makes or breaks a work, right?

The dot on The i —

that was the title. The idea never graduated, and the story morphed, or maybe it was i.

"Professor? Hi," I said. I couldn't get through the gate and up the stairs fast enough. It's hot as hell and anyway I hate when people watch me like I'm on parade. This one's ok, though, so no sweat.

"Jenny, nice to see you, come on in. Come in," Professor Caufield said, wrinkled, worn, but just the same old Caufield, with ideals. Though, weird, I know—married and with a girl now.

Turns out, we all recover from given Life blows and momentary infamy. Somehow, as long as we get up. They're living a quiet life, even with the book publishing, and multiple editions, and all. Now, you mention "Catcher" down the block and almost nobody knows what the jackass you're talking about. Caufield says *nobody* reads. That's not true, obviously, because you do, and I do. I even know the old Robert Burns poem, and the forgone misunderstanding:

[First Setting]
Comin thro' the rye, poor body,
    Comin thro' the rye,
She draigl't a' her petticoatie
    Comin thro' the rye.

[CHORUS.]
        Oh Jenny 's a' weet poor body
            Jenny 's seldom dry,
        She draigl't a' her petticoatie
            Comin thro' the rye.

I've read enough yarns to blanket the family my mom says, "...maybe, but just what did you understand, honey, I'll never be quite sure..."

I chose Jenny.

I even looked it up. It means *white wave*. I don't know why but it reminds me more of extinction than starting again. Something like a verb, rather than a noun, to jenny— it makes me think of the way an ordinary undyed waxed candle is snuffed half-way. It's like the variations on a theme of white, that never really is, white, I mean. It leaves that lingering trace, of the archaic poetry, in the un-scent-ed— an old smoke's tale. I feel those shades of gray, seriously, like a population of ghost sensations.

It's a shrinking population. White folk, I mean, are dying out. I feel kinda responsible.

"They're here!"

Caufield has always been sort of an idol growing up. I'm not here for that though. Holdan's ok and isn't going say dumb things like "don't do what I wouldn't do."

Life is not a game. We know that.

It's confirmation.

There was quite a fussing and shuffling as they tumbled downstairs. They chose Seamour.

"You didn't look it up?" I said in disbelief.

"Nope, it just fucking fits. I mean, c'mon, my parents picked Tabitha, for chrissakes," you said pressing lips together like its fact if you say so.

I've been whooped a few times with the Bible, so I know Tabitha is the one St. Peter raised from the dead. I guess it's trivia in the end. It's a cool name, though. I almost took it, but I didn't want them to feel all weirded out about it, like we were becoming mirror twins, or something black lodge Lynchian.

I still feel odd about the clothes you gave me. It's not because these are thrift store. I'm glad to see them.

"Do I look ok" I said, tugging at the lilac floral hem a little. I ask this so often I've started leaving out the question mark. It's a hallmark of my insecurity—my social statement. I know they're going to say yes. I mean, it's *Seamour*, right?

"Did you put your soul strap on today?" they joke, and I have to smile, crookedly. My wisdom teeth have wreaked havoc on my money-makers. Seriously, poor people used to sell their teeth so rich people could implant them. I'm not even sure there was good anesthesia back then. It's vile.

Modern folks sell plasma.

I knew a poor unemployed blind guy who sold plasma to Uber their three-year-old to free pre-school. There were too many on the bus for *that one* to be picked up. Right.

"Yeah," I said.

They've got work brand jeans on, with the goddam label on the outside. I hate that. I'm not even going to give that brand "name." Why? why, I just don't get it, would a company do that. Companies are run by people though sometimes I wonder. Maybe it's like in that movie where you have to put special sunglasses on to see the Aliens.

I suppose I shouldn't pay so much attention to our labels, and names.

I know, I know, sticks and stones and all, but words and names matter. A kick in the crotch hurts even if it's tangential.

I like Seamour.

Even if the name doesn't 100% fit.

"Are you sure you still want to go out?" Tabitha said at the door.

Maybe that was the beginning, though it obviously started way before that. That's what they said, later, in the hospital.

"Yeah," I said. "Let's go."

1. Wayback

Guess we'll always be searching with a torch or candelabra, flashlight or laser beam, for that all elusive "Big Bang."

The Beginning— I mean of whatever it is that we're tracing. It's why the Bible is still BIG after all these centuries. Not for morality. No, for the conceptual misgiving.

The Genesis.

Yeah, you got me on that one. It is also part of why I chose Jenny.

That phonic variant is graphed from the Japanese, a feminine forename meaning "Spring." And to be sure, I wobbled, between G and J. Ultimately, I pinned J as you see.

You'll say of course, ugh, Jesus Christ.

But nope. J is the tenth letter of the alphabet and is derived from the Phoenician, one of the earliest languages in which the letter, as such, did not yet exist, though need for it apparently did. It sounds as a juh and yuh.

Variably written out as Y or i, and later formed as J. Hence, the archaic Yeshua. It is also strikingly in character, a letter that in certain foreign tongues disappears, in a breath, as in Spanish as a mere Hhhhuh— exhale— though not as invisible as an H itself. And sometimes the J and G cannot be differentiated in sound at all.

Like in Jenny.

G is the seventh letter, and ties too close to God and to that all elusive good. In my eye. Blocked, even typographically, the horizontal bar forming a sort of trap. But J is a seat I can sit myself on, a hook even, to hold me, if need be. And 10 likewise is the more wholesome number for a person.

It's the number of self-determination.

See how 10 has, in itself, the Everything and the Nothing. The binary code. It is after all our virtual reality.

My speech therapist said in Life independence is better than perfection. I disagree marginally and Seamour summed it better for me in the cafeteria saying: *independence within interdependence is perfection itself.*

That balance beam poise which the organism of all biology is craving.

So, I guess maybe all this pivoted with our middle school teacher, Phae— and it wasn't Mrs. or Ms. or Mr.

We were horrified, and in awe, and, and well, just fascinated. Cuz how could you pave your own persona like that? Out here, in suburbia of mid-middle America with flat plains of uniformity.

—Big Stars go by first name.

I should hurry up to mention that of course Tabitha and I had known each other since we were like five. And we'd always been as if enamored with the Theatre of the Absurd. We just didn't know what to call it back then.

The waiting.

Like for Godot.

But it was in fifth grade, on the very first day of September, that our homeroom teacher, garbed in flowered knee socks, dusty blue bicycle shorts, non-descript neutral tank, pink Hello Kitty hoodie, and tie-dyed babushka, stepped forward, pointed to the board at letters that may very well have been Greek or hieroglyph to us, and said in a lilt:

"Hi classs, my name is Phae. My pronoun's they/ them, and we are going to ssskip the ice breaker."

A universal wave of relief covered the room. Whatever the pronoun, we all melted— feeling immediately understood. Somehow safe, in our own person.

Seamour has since explained it better than I. There is something in the mindset of Admin that perpetuates this strict enforcement of hierarchy. The breaking of horses, they call it. Seamour did, I mean. Administration explains nothing.

It does. The break, and the breaks.

Ice breakers are designed to break our barriers down, and "facilitate" social interaction. Do I have to point out the bully-pulp?

My dad went to church every Sunday, for reasons unarticulated, and criticized liberally, beginning with reproach of the Forced Meet when the Pastor obsequiously began each service with "Welcome to the House of God," proceeding next in asking everyone to "now turn and greet your neighbor." Farcical smiles, the pressing of the flesh, and retraction of everyone back into their guilt-ridden sleeves. Except of course those for whom it was all redundant, having already given the nod or smile of polite acknowledgement to fellow human being— having the *house of God* in the sanctuary of their heart— not in any Pastor's parish atrium. *That* was Dad's first domestic quarrel.

So, yeah. We thought, sure, this is going to be a critical year.

Phae floated around the aisles with assorted colored papers, glue sticks, and black washable markers: "Pleassse, and thank you, write or draw Something to decorate OUR room... something you'd like to see thiss school year."

I can hear the snickers from the back far corner.

We all knew fifth grade is the Year of Sex Ed, and I fully expected that Ricky, christened with that "tricky" handicap of a name, would go and draw something caricatured, pornographic, and self-deprecatory. Oddly, it was also the year slated for Camp, a weekend-long test for home separation anxiety...

I ended up making a collaged folded newspaper stack, surrounded by black hawks and torn-out hornets. Our local teams. Not bees. Not birds. Basketball. Seamour took one look then and suppressed a smile:

"Looks like we know where your mind went!"

Right, I mean Tabitha, who had a big smear of black marker, like a puddle, spread with spit I think, and ambiguous poofs above, glued into a hunched green giant. Like some thought-bubbles hovering across the construction-paper.

"Yeah, and uh, you looking forward to getting your period?" I cracked. Tabitha matured early. Later they confided that that had happened in fourth grade.

"It's Long Lake, dumb ass."

The tree canopies had no trunks, yet. Just leaves. Eyes roamed around the room a bit and we settled into the pleasant and anti-invasive task.

Meanwhile, in a calm drawl Phae carried on about expectations, class rules, common bureaucracy, and all that lends to monotone sense of safety.

We zoned out.

When I was a toddler, I had a weighted blankie. In later years, I saw Thunder Shirts for dogs on TV. It's quite similar in feel. This atmosphere. I suspect we're seeking out the womb all our life.

Security of physical containment within adopted boundaries of self.

Arms.

So back to the beginning. The trigger. Seamour says it was when they divided us, boy and girl.

I said, "O! Adam and the rib?" jumping the gun.

But Tabitha actually meant in Health Class, during that aforementioned, Human Growth and Dev., component. Yeah, I couldn't understand it either when Mrs. Benjamin had said, "The ladies will now leave the classroom and gather for the following study unit in the Gymnasium." While boys were to stay in the Auditorium.

And I... I went to hide in the bathroom.

A stupid thoughtless error.

On my heels, Derrick. I turned around. No beating around the bush.

"What's up, Cunt?" Derrick pinched my cheek, brushing passed me. I was at that rotund interval of puberty. I'm sure you've noticed that everyone has their lean and fat years, preteen to twenties and again in thirties, by whatever degree of extreme. Joys of young adulthood. Probably continues infinitum.

Derrick was several grades up, maybe eighth. It doesn't matter.

You know Rock Hudson?

That kind of build. But not as nice.

People so often seem surprised. What?! Rock, no way! —on hearing that the dude was a closet homosexual —then disdain, for the roundness around the body's edges, and wait a minute, sure since you've mentioned now, on second thought, that babyface. Oh, yeah, uh huh, uh huh. See it? But polite doubt ever circling the beautiful ladies Greta Garbo, Marlena Dietrich or Joan Crawford.

Maybe increasingly less now a days.

Not that I was questioning orientations. At that point, I mean.

I'm leaping ahead of myself in the story— and it's not about me. I changed course and ducked into the dim library. Coast clear. Nobody manning the circulation desk. The head clerk, Mr. Bateman, must've been somewhere around shelving books on hands and knees. Bateman, behind adult backs, going by nickname of "Master-Bateman." Middle school humor— any name like that was creative fodder. I rounded the stacks, cautious to avoid Bateman or any assistants.

And Seamour was there.

I mean Tabitha. Crying.

2. philosophy

In my High School personal notes, I'd written:

There is perhaps no greater art than that of self-discipline. Self-discipline is an enormous task in itself; and is comparatively simpler than correcting or guiding others.

Good intentions alone do not suffice in providing acceptable instruction in proper conduct. To demand, without discouraging—to dissuade, without destroying— is indeed a delicate matter.

The small me, compromising every undisciplined ego, is endangered by the correction of others— (who is So, or So, to tell me...?). The small me sees only itself, and others, as a huddled mass of other little me's, self-absorbed and self-serving, and caught between the constant conformist pleas of me too, me too, and the incessant demand for individuality:

Hey, what about me?

Indeed, a great force is needed to rise above, to overcome, and be able to see the self as an active power: I.

I am responsible, I am able, I can, I will...

And of course, this mere recognition is not enough to ensure a moral direction of action. It is the first step towards self-discipline and is critical in the advent of discipline in others— enabling others to undertake the personal responsibility that will make possible future correction, which can only come through self-conviction.

The question remains, who is to provide guidance in a sound moral direction?

To be able to learn from the mistakes of others is undoubtedly an ability few of us possess. Others have made their mistakes, then why can't I??? regresses the not fully disciplined mind. I want, and I can, does not mean one should... here, it would seem, to truly attain self-discipline, a person must relinquish more of the individual I, to embrace an abstract oneness, in which things, beings, and activity, are guided not by wants and abilities, but by needs and merits...

— I didn't keep a diary.

That was the dry opening to the Magnum Opus I had started second to last year. The further premise, the attentive reader will Gestalt, in reference to the title given earlier, was to be an illustration of how the I developed in relation to the other… and the space balanced between. Hence the crucial "Dot" on.

"— Hey, you ok?" I asked, kicking myself in the ass for the stupid but inevitable question, not wanting to preemptively shutdown response by blurting: "Oh my god what's wrong?!"

Like, what isn't? would have been my response.

Tabitha launched into a lot of nose blowing, and I scolded myself for my anxiety over our cover likewise being blown. I mean my friend was in obvious distress, and needed help, not self-centered over-conscious nagging for cutting class. I took a breath and settled into full lotus. I waited. Seamour later told me how that always creeped them out. I've learned since that hyper-mobility is strongly correlated to Autism and other neurodivergence.

Not that I've been diagnosed.

But back to March of that year. It turned out Mrs. Benjamin had somehow impressed the group of

"Ladies," as to the "Specialness of their bodies," and Tabitha construed this as Socially sanctioned Whoredom.

Seamour explained it to me this way, between wiping eyes and nose. In a word: "Exchange."

By which it was understood that we were all bringing certain play pieces. Bargaining chips. That social-relations were seldom, if ever, without that inky squid-like creature called Quid Pro Quo. Even in families. Children after all, in history, once born, were born to aid the family in the work of survival. Many hands make work lighter is the hand me down Mother Goosed expression, and its slight traces remain in the modern fam.

Mrs. Benjamin, I imagine, was a cheerleader way back. Having broken age 40, all the fine lines could no longer be filled in with any ordinary foundation. Tabitha said that face must have been plastered with makeup from early elementary. There were permanent cracks on a "good egg," that now wore a pasted-on, well-practiced, quasi-effortless smile which looked more like a well-chiseled "high art" mask. You know.

Cultured.

Like cheese.

The smile expressing a learned disapproval.

Disappointment.

Benjamin was an enforcer of rules. At the slightest infraction. Like if you walked too slow, and paused in confusion at the Order to "hurry up," Ole Benji's affected affection dropped into an immaculately painted frown:

"*That's* recess *with me!*" sharply pronounced.

Like a win. Sometimes accompanied by a snap of the fingers. A satisfaction that I just could not understand. Vampirical, like taking from a young person's free time would add, or I dunno, subtract, something of the years elapsed, for the bag.

The catching of prey made Benjamin stand taller, all of about 4' 9, and I noticed the fitted cable knit over sadly padded hoisted boobs, long gold necklace, carefully coordinating earrings, belt, and pump buckles, and the laboriously coiffed, red-dyed hairdo starched precisely into position. The effect, one of being put together. A real professional woman. Presumably unlike us slobs who couldn't even walk the plank when told.

I've never actually understood those tunes, where a woman croons on and on and on about feeling or being a woman. Huh? Like what is the back-story. Anyway—

Benji knew how to do what's told, and better, how to tell you what to do. A reliable trooper. It was sort of like the confidence of a $100 bill in a leather wallet. Crumpled and deflated, on the streets, it still has purchase power.

Benjamin was thoroughly chauvinist. Age, gender, or ability. When I say chauvinist, I mean, it was like Benjamin was flag bearer for all those identifiers that are not at all worked on, but a person is born into. Meritless.

I think it's called Privilege.

I imagine Benji had maybe grown up as one of those highly motivated so-called helpers, like in younger classrooms or resource rooms, where status and advantage are ever present, yet understated. Subtle power moves. Select or self-appointed ambassadors who say "hiiiii," as if to everybody, and lavish big pageant smiles on some, slip in candy, discriminatingly, and bestow hugs on a chosen few (those who don't slouch or drool), notably those who cannot very well say no (*though they sometimes do, and that natural response is considered irrational, and rude).

Because this outreach was commonly called "Being Nice."

I've watched peers like Charlie, Amanda and others, aspiring to that most generous social poise, and something felt wrong. Unhealthy. Looking at it I wish it were otherwise. It might more aptly be labeled as appropriating a special treatment, noting the get-out-of-class-free card and social regard that comes with that show of public Philanthropy.

Seamour wasn't like that: "Being nice."

Seamour *was*. Kind. To everybody, the same. Not pushy. Without interest in eventual gains, real or potential. It's why they were upset about "favors." Owing somebody something, that is what a *favor* is based on. I go ahead and do something "nice" for you, on credit, and now you have some debit to pay. Undefined. In time, scope, or duration.

"That can be called in *anytime*," says Seamour. And you don't know what it is.

They particularly balked at female favors, and all the preening and covering up and misty euphemizing. What Seamour referred to as the Sexual Economy. And, here, I need to elaborate on their position. It's not what you might think.

Oldest profession... may have jumped to mind. It did for me, with trepidation. But Tabitha said, wait, the question is, is it honest?

In non-coerced prostitution, the situation is clear. As I understood it. I mean, there is a service, a price, and a fee rendered. ...but if it's a *favor*, there may, or may not be service, or repayment. What there is, for almost definitely sure, is loathing and resentment. Expectation. Met, or unmet. And very likely, some kind of violence. Internalized, or externalized.

Coercion. Of self or others.

As Seamour called it, "Domestic Prostitution." Victim and perpetrator, intertwined as if one and the same, user and used, depending on where we happen to stop-action within the animation. Complicit. Co-dependent.

Ever the extremist, Seamour said, with one last blow of the nose: "If I ever get hitched, no one is going to work for my ass."

3. Bonding

Introduced to us, in these middling years, was also the system of work. A systematic working for— a Program, as in "Curricular." Notice that I am dancing around calling it a system of rewards. Seamour took this hard, as irrational. By our final year, I sensed a strong, as if communal tendency. At least with me. We shared. Everything.

I was exaggerating, though. We didn't know each other since we were 5. I'd been shuffled around too much moving in the school system since infancy— daycare, then Preschool, then pre-K, Kindergarten and the whole twelve yards. I was considered extra young, too. Qualifying for that "advantageous," depending how you might look at it, program called Young Fives Admissions— with my birthday falling neatly between the requisite window of June 1st and December 1st.

I can't remember when we met exactly now. Dammit.

I guess I've felt like we've always known each other, from some time, before. Before either of us was born.

But back to that system of rewards. The Working4 program, as I'll call it.

It evolved with our generation. It used to be a thing selectively implemented in Special Education. But on being received with broad sweeping approbation, the technique soon enough became mainstream. Now, everybody walks around carrying a folder with their name on it and stickies of some sort (Velcro, repositionable vinyls, actual stickers, or what-have-you).

It's very simple. If you're not already familiar.

There's a printed affirmation.

I AM WORKING FOR _________________.

Now, you might balk, and say Satisfaction! for a job well done, or Self-respect.

Pride.

But it's quite primal.

I want to say primitive.

"You're offending the indigenous," says Seamour. Ironically, and I know why.

It's very similar to beads. The folder commonly says, *working for Skittles… or working for Chips… or Tablet… or Bike ride…*

Scratch those visuals.

—Minus the typed out affirmative sentence.

—Swap out flimsy plastic folder for briefcase, purse, or wallet—

—And Viola!

The most of us are working for: dollars.

Pennies, even.

So, if you're thinking, well, we can "elevate" the endgame, uh, can we really? Differently abled, is all.

"*Well,* what are you working for, hon?"

Seamour looked at the guidance counselor eye to eye the first time it was officially opened to us in sixth grade, and shut the folder unblinkingly:

"Condoms."

Doubtlessly, you've heard that kids are developing seemingly faster and faster, even as our life expectancy, theoretically, is rising worldwide to a whopping 70 years of age.

"And you," icy eyes turning.

"...Forrr.... me," I let out slowly.

"That's not an option," looking at us both sternly, "You're *either* working for snacks, *or* toys. Take your pick... Or it will be picked for you."

"T-t-toys," I said blushing, having caught Seamour's raised eyebrow, a little wicked curve pulling on our mouths instantaneously. Then wiped. Both of us, idiotically, filling in "what kind of toys."

In context.

Middle school minds, spontaneous, you know. And imaginary. None of us was serious.

"Do I need to contact home that neither of you are taking the WORK4 incentive seriously?"

Nooooo....

And not for fear, but for humiliation. Nobody at home took it serio. It was, for both of us, met with scorn and disdain.

Whatever happened to intrinsic motivation? Character development...? Dad sneered the year before on receiving the info packet.

"You're working to conform. Or not," Seamour said afterward, succinctly.

What we determined, then, was to be as knowledgeable about things as possible. I hesitate to say "Smart." Somebody might take offense that it's about intelligence. What we had decided was that it was about exposure. Experience, real or secondhand, or even as fantasy, just so an informed choice could be made. Even if based only on our long thought-out personal opinion.

 A relationship between you and your decision.

It was about that time we had "the Talk." Amongst ourselves. Seamour was dead set against. I mean Tabitha.

"Bring another person??? into this shit?"

What about motherhood? I mean, "...isn't that like the basic purpose of every living body?"

"To be fucked? Easy for you to say."

I obviously wouldn't be carrying. Maybe that's what makes me curious, the improbability.

"They're working on male surrogates," I offered biting down on my chapped lip.

Silence.

Maybe they should work harder. I thought about my Mom and Dad. It's a strange miracle that they found time between arguing and all to make up thoroughly like that to bring a new life— and Mom being on an IUD. Around 99% effective, or so I've heard.

That makes me 1% I suppose.

"There must be other purpose," Seamour said, "Not every body has babies."

Right there. Some people can't, not by choice. And it occurred to me that infertility is seemingly an ever- increasing issue in modern times. We've reached some impasse. Like Nature itself is "declining." A part of humanity anyway.

Seamour's extended family, big in itself, also has several adoptees. I don't know how they do it. I think it's a noble thing, taking in someone with no family, but I'd be afraid of my own flesh and blood turning, never mind a stranger. I've seen the hate people try to hide against those closest to them— when they feel for whatever reason, factually or fictionally, that they are being repressed.

It occurred to me what hell would be, for me.

I've never been in detention of any sort, criminally. But I've heard they keep strict account of pencils, and pens are forbidden. Apparently, the innards can be shaped into key picks. For handcuffs.

The idea that I might not have access to a writing implement and paper sickened me, on the thought of it. No outlet. Suddenly that seemed worse than a locked door. Worse than starvation.

Worse than No Exit.

A book can be an escape into another space, and I hesitate to say it, but I think I could live without—just subsist on my own imagination. Trying to force it to greater extent. Maybe. But having nothing with which to write, or to draw, or to sculpt, or to make anything, that would fundamentally undermine who I am.

It would steal that vital dot.

No, the lack would reach in, crush my spirit, and leave nothing.

It would be death.

Or maybe I would try to learn to sing... or perfect contortionism, or otherwise push my body as the only medium left...?

Then, Seamour said:

"That wasn't what I meant. I meant we are born fucked."

I note there that it wasn't "you." Plural or single.

Only "We."

I didn't even want to think about hell for Tabitha. I mean whatever it was, I never wanted Seamour to have to experience that depravity.

4. differences

It was the time we saw Phae in blue jeans that struck us dumb, near year's end. Field day. It was the way the skinny jeans wrapped around the thigh and fitted the curve. Up till that point, I think it's fair to say, we thought the odds weighed in with certain bias: the hairy legs, the deflated chest, the colorless face.

The balance tipped towards the masculine.

Sitting on the rocks by the fence we glanced at each other intently.

It's moments like these that you recognize people you mesh with, or not. Being in agreement isn't the thing, as much as picking up on a certain wave of thought, a question in the atmosphere that doesn't need to be spoken to tilt the direction of the conversation. Maybe we took it for granted.

If we were strangers, it would have likely been Omfg! Are you reading my thinking... Or are we thinking the Same Thing?

Synapsis.

"What do you think they are rejecting?"

It was like all of a sudden our differences surfaced, when we'd tried really hard all this time to push them out to neutral.

...Rightly, or wrongly, for the moment of perception, one of us (as a group) it seemed was being forsaken, in pursuit of the other "skin," as it were... as Phae transitioned.

"I don't know," they said. "I want to say it doesn't matter."

"But does it?" I wondered, "Not liking who you are?"

"Let's not be negative. Maybe 'not liking who you are,' is really, 'trying to better who you are'...?"

We sat with that discomfort.

It was that summer that Tabitha said: "Let's make a pact—we don't divide by pronoun."

Seamour's sensitive like that. Humanitarian.

I wasn't sure what it would mean for us, the ambiguity. I pictured Phae, hovering in-between, like an abstract demilitarized ground. I wanted to believe that it ends here. On not this, and not that.

On a leveling of contention. That *we* wanted to be Human. Motivated without interest. Trying to find that good Setzhaun, when it seemed all the world was frantic to brothelize, and sell out their half.

"Done." I said, our eyes locking in sincerity.

It's always more complicated than that. But I feel really strongly about resolution— in the moment. So, it was final, but not conclusive. Not definitive, but working on understanding...

It took us through all of puberty.

In those beginnings, I was still trying to understand why my Dad died, and why I couldn't tell Tabitha. The end of the school year was pressing on, and I'd stopped taking care of myself, unwittingly, in those long dark cold months of illness. Dad didn't eat. Couldn't. It was the nature of the illness, to systematically shut down the metabolism, in a slow insidious way, as the liver decays. Silently. ...I'd also stopped eating regularly, and no, it wasn't showing, yet. Turns out you can be round and mal-nutritioned. The body goes into starvation mode before weight shifts, and it acts promptly on the brain. You stop seeing yourself.

Minimalism in chaos became a way.

Not a Tao but a Don't.

I felt so depressive in the fading of life— Dad's— that even when I did ingest something, say an apple, it came right back up. Self-rejected. Eating disorders aren't always about the kind of Vanity we'd presume.

...*Why they?* Aidan Ware had ventured to ask Phae one morning, a few weeks in. Boldly.

"I'm non-binary. That means I do not identify as either a man or woman."

I think we all pictured a genital hydra. Or maybe an empty slate. A baby born with genetic mutation. I dare not say defect, because that'll be read as uncompassionate. Trying to wrap a mind around it felt like looking in one of those carnival mirrors. The long and the short, and the one that projects copies of you all over the place.

"If you want help visualizing, picture me with a mouse in my pocket. You'd refer to us as *They*."

No one let out a peep. Fourth grade probably would have giggled. Or eighth, guffawed. Meanly.

"Of course," Seamour said at lunch. "Aren't we all a spaceship of organisms?"

"So, everybody should be 'They'?"

Shrug: "Parasites."

But I think it set a brain worm loose for Tabitha.

We had talks about God.

I said God is neither. Tabitha, claiming "both."

We tried hard to picture Phae— not identifying as either male or female. Not both. It puzzled. I guess I didn't really want to see God as Phae-like. Maybe Seamour didn't want to see Phae as God-like. Maybe we all just want a respectable distance.

Space.

Tabitha had a headache and pressed left thumb, then right thumb to the third eye— that vague indentation just above the bridge of the nose where the eyebrows divide. In Chinese medicine, it's that acupressure point called Yin Tang. The third eye is an interesting thing. We think of it as being there upon the forehead. Sometimes, it's represented in Ancient or Modern art as a sideways eye. Usually horizontal, though.

It has significance, spiritually, as providing insight. Extrasensory perception. And people meditate on that third eye point to gain higher states of consciousness. Wisdom.

The All Seeing Eye of God.

What's interesting is that it's suggested that there really is a physical third eye— or its remnants. Something like the appendix. Vestige. Within the Pineal Gland. Think reptilian brain, and theories of evolution. Reptiles and amphibians have a third parietal eye. Linked to corresponding endocrine gland that senses light and works to maintain their circadian rhythm (you know, for sleep) and for regulating body temperature.

Mammals don't have one anymore—anymore, being the key word.

Our Therapsid relatives did.

Arms and legs appeared, eventually, and upright posture. According to theory. The third eye, under the skin incidentally in case you're not visualizing, diminished overtime entirely into the pineal gland.

But Seamour would warn: "People look down on Madame Blavatsky."

As esoteric.

So, I probably shouldn't even bother to mention it. Blavatsky being a co-founder of Theosophy. That was a deliberate attempt in the Western mind to blend Religion, Philosophy, and Science. Frankly, I don't much see the difference. I mean, I do, superficially. But really, it's all human thought, isn't it??

That's maybe what grounded our choices as years went on. Tabitha and I didn't see much difference. I mean of course, there were differences, but there were ninety times as many things we had in common. With the world, with each other. Our Humanity.

I suppose it was in internal revolt that we started switching out our visible social attributes. It happened gradually, though in hindsight, it's immediate. Looking into a telescope. Something like the effect of light years. The precedent was laid open when Seamour refused to borrow my new Junior Varsity jacket in the Fall. Basketball. The grossed-out expression told me everything I need not ask.

Distain.

Tabitha gestured an empty hand towards Vicky and Mike. I suppose as "classic" example.

Yeah, I could see for myself the proud Varsity pussies draped in their leading man's coattails. Sire and Bitch, each staking a claim in the social convention of status ownership.

Tethered to the same tired old line.

It disgusted Tabitha as much as it did me, way back when we were still tots. As middle schoolers.

We weren't children anymore and we weren't going to kid ourselves that something had become alright suddenly. It took a minute, continuing to irk at our conscience. That's when Seamour said as a highfalutin dare:

"What if we tested the scene by switching *all* our accoutrements?"

All of them. It'd mean hardship. Big and foreign as the word.

Ostracization.

"A test of character," Seamour said, set.

Character.

Suddenly I saw us as actors in a play.

And no, it shouldn't make a difference. We didn't have lines. Scripted. Like in some stereotypical coming of age primetime after school special.

We would refuse.

We'd carved out our names in the Sycamore tree of Arnold's parking lot a while ago. To make it more concrete. Letting loose our old names— into the Infinite. Shucked, temporary shells. It sounds trite now. Heartbreaking even. As a kind of satire, we outlined our assumed novelty with a broken heart. A crass parody, as anti-statement of fools in love:

Jenny & Seamour.

I was only mildly surprised to recognize, well after, that no one'd called me by my given name for years— without falter. As if I had previously been unnamed or something. Not even my mother.

Caufield slipped up a bit then and again, with the occasional "Tab" or "Tabitha," and then, much clearing of the throat until dropping nomenclature altogether. Funny thing, though, Seamour's father never had any trouble calling me "Jenny," and I took that as a win.

I'd picked well.

Or maybe it's easier, talking, calling, and name dropping, when it's not your flesh and blood congealing.

[CHORUS.]
Oh Jenny 's a' weet poor body
Jenny 's seldom dry,
She draigl't a' her petticoatie
Comin thro' the rye.

It's somebody else's dirty laundry.

So, we were already all in, and that summer before High School I boxed up my clothes, pausing at my boxers. But hell, if everything, then, here it is... and I'd have a similar "oh hell" on the receiving end. Panties, hose, slips, brassieres— even a random push up bra. I didn't know Tabitha had one.

Okay, so we had to compromise on the shoes.

Guess it wasn't exactly Cinderella.

It was startling, as far as sizes went otherwise, the girth of hip matched my waistline, and somehow everything hung fashionably on Seamour, a little loose or a little snug, but chic like on a department store display figure. I guess on average, we were about the same size, give or take, regardless of difference of shape, evidenced by full or empty cups, bulging or not underdrawers.

As a fact we could've omitted the undergarments, (who would know?), but the experiment would have been less honest. Right? Or at least, we'd have felt the lesser for it.

Like we had backed down.

But try as I could, I could not fit into any one of the boots or sneakers. Even the flip flops and slippers didn't have enough length of sole to walk on, cutting into my heel.

"Loafer shopping?" Seamour joked.

Neither of us was shoe crazy, God bless. We drew the mark there, and kept to our own. I guarantee nobody noticed. And, if we hadn't started when we did, early teen, it's unlikely that the noonday shadow would also go mostly unnoticed, later.

As it did, mostly.

Because of course as time went on, so did the hormonal Biological clock. We promptly outgrew sets of play clothes. Call us obstinate, but we refused to budge from the challenge. Some things last for a very long time. But when a thing had to be replaced, it was.

Like for like.

I imagine my father rolling around. Laughing.

Had Dad been alive, I doubt I would have agreed to this little vivi-socio-emotional experiment. People talk high and all, of "we the people," and about "good human beings," but when it comes right down to it, there's that ingrained fear of social disappointment. Inherent.

The Order.

Whatever it is we're born into.

That stratification.

That the good Lord made distinct members for a reason. But, Seamour asked, pertinently:

"Where does it say, in the Bible, to exacerbate the differences?" No, seems it says quite explicitly, and after much strife: "Love one another as I have loved you."

As I have loved you. Without qualification.

And we understood that it had everything and nothing to do with Sex.

Coming through the Rye.

[Second Setting]
Gin a body meet a body, comin thro' the rye,
Gin a body kiss a body, need a body cry;
Ilka body has a body, ne'er a ane hae I;
But a' the lads they loe me, and what the waur am I.

5. the Thing

Of course, it didn't.

We'd climbed behind the strip mall. There was an outcropping of rocks that made a natural invitation. Maybe the heap of hillside was left by "lack of funds." Otherwise, hard to explicate the odd randomness of the excavation. It was a bump in what was the strip-mall'd belly of the local Business Residential Zoning area. There was a haircutting place, a Meet n' Greet deli and cheap coffee type hangout, some tax accountant's hut, and other obscure offices of So and So's.

All tapering off into ignonimity... and beyond these abandoned factories like headstones marked the periphery of our city banks.

On top of this mound was a plateau that sloped inward. Not quite a basin dent, but water could in theory, pool. I mean in a deluge or something. In any case, it dipped like a sunken bellybutton on a distended stomach, so that on scaling the front, people or animals would be swiftly swallowed, in perspective, and made invisible.

Inconsequential.

We were curious. That's all I can say.

We found no one but us there. Rocks loosely strewn. Vestiges of footpaths. Blocks. Abandoned construction. Effort, overtaken by vegetation.

The Nature of things.

Overgrowth and undergrowth.

We had struggled a bit getting to this point and landed hand in hand pulling each other up, slipping periodically on loosened dirt. Letting go was a tangible thing. Sweat lingering in a strange silent exchange. There was a wild stand of trees at the far end. Deciduous, and these stood up right like startled hair on end.

A bristling brown and gray tabby we'd roused from sleep.

A slice of moon was visible against the cobalt horizon. As a sort of scythe head, hanging over us, midday. The blade ready to tumble down on us in our hometown. Unlikely precision, and the curve of my mouth twisted in grim mimicry. I smoothed that wayward lilac hem. It had a way of curling up obnoxiously. Needed ironing, and I suppose in a common paperback it would been adjectived as the suggestive lift of the dress or something of the sort, poetically, peeping tom vulgar. "Revealing."

The rest of the world seemed far.

Its problems lying on our hearts.

To be different.

You see how strange that is. The language is the same, but not the intent: to be different, from divisiveness. As in, to be "more one." I could see us lying down, resting, elbows up, propping our craniums and star gazing. Emptying our minds. But we didn't.

Relax I mean.

Maybe we would have thought about getting away. No cars between us. Buses enough round here in our small city. And a person can always walk.

Right?

Loaded that expression. I've felt the weight of people walking out.

Walk.

That's what they say when you get away with a crime. Not really though.

Away.

Seamour patted a rock, and I sat, pulling the 8oz from my pocket. I twisted the cap and offered. Tabitha took a grateful sip, small at first and then a thirsty swig. I watched the way the throat worked, that smooth rhythm of skin slipping. Our knuckles touched and I could feel the passing through, a living force.

Water.

I capped up our bottle and it gave a spent crinkle, releasing easily in my grasp.

We were both touchy. Seamour annoyed.

Heated.

But a the lads they loe me, and what the waur am I.

Gin a body meet a body, comin frae the town,
Gin a body kiss a body, need a body gloom;
Ilka Jenny has her Jockey, ne'er a ane hae I,
But a' the lads they loe me, and what the waur am I.

Waur means worse, in case you're wondering.

Funny thing is I picked Jenny without reference to the poem running through my mind. It occurred to me later. The reference, I mean.

A jockey is a master, riding you with a whip.

I can't remember what they were saying. By now the day was getting late and the sun was turning to molasses.

"I was trying to get a rise out of you."

"And it worked," I responded in a huff, and not in the way the words were meant.

We'd been talking about the so-called Jewish question. Because the Bible does mention a Chosen People. My family, as it were. Rumored anyway, with extra shroud of mystery.

"You have a Jew in your family, closer than you think," is what Dad said.

It never failed to upset me. The not knowing. I'll note that every Peoples have their high and low moments in history collectively. I just didn't know. When you don't know your family, and you're hypochondriac, like me, you wonder what kind of ills and past sins, or contra wise, what worthy accomplishments are running through your splattered blood.

Seamour's lineage was neat and tidy, so far as we could see. Everything hung in proper Bourgeoise order of heirloom. Tracing heritage was doable by papeterie, in the form of marriage licenses, and birth certificates, etc. Whatever old Caulfield's rebellion had been worth, it'd resulted mostly in an elaboration on Tradition.

The mess on my side left everything sorely open to question. Must be nice to have a family tree. That's a delusion, though. Blood relation has nothing to do with bond, in the positive sense. I guess I was angry. Ok maybe I was envious. Whatever. I want to be open and honest about it. In truth, I had been carrying this hard on for a while.

Belonging.

That's a beautiful word. I can't help it, but I see that one word as an entire micro poem.

It's the pull of magnets. They exist separately. Yet drawing near, the connection is already made, even without the crash on touching. The one that happens, as it must, if you get too close. Present tense, and future implied as well, breaking up the parts—To be, to long.

To. Not with.

I want to say it had nothing to do with Tabitha, or Seamour. It's as if my thoughts were pre-empted. Into crisis...

"It's Timing."

"You mean that things happen in sequence?"

"No."

By that time, we were done. Spent.

Our clothes intertangled in a consummate pile, belonging to the both of us. Seamour, below, breasts flattened under as my half-body shielded our partial nudity from spying invisible raptors.

Withdrawal— having blundered this far— was farthest thing from my frantic mind. And Tabitha had said nothing. Maybe we weren't committed. Maybe it was, in reversal, a point to prove.

Rebellion in rebellion.

Maybe fucking Nature took over.

We won't know.

Seamour launched into abstract wondering on the mechanics of reality. We'd come back to the present, later. There was no hurt, nor blame, or self-deprecation. Unspoilt.

"Situations are dynamic. Layered. Not at all sequential, as in cause-n-effect."

"Parallel cause and effect?" I said half assed.

"Exactly."

We paused. Skin to skin. The breeze and the sun luxuriating. The world felt peaceful. Good.

"Like say if a woman gets wet on hearing another woman, in an adjacent aisle of the grocery store laugh, the conclusion might be 'lesbo,' right?"

Seamour's weird like that, but I humored the social scientist. "...Just time of day, then? ...no direct correlation you mean...?" I said sitting up, and wondering about comedic timing, wryly.

"Circumstantial."

We were also circumstance then.

It was late, not quite dark. We slipped back into our tenting. I mean each other's clothes. I passed them their flannel, for a moment remembering *this is my big shirt*. I could feel its warmth, and softness, worn in by us... it had been way oversized for starters. Huge. I got it for Christmas. A woven blue-red-green plaid with raglan sleeves. Seamour pulled and put it on, looking through me, through the neck opening, not exactly at me.

With ease.

Fitted.

Those shitty work-brand jeans, a deep rich blue. The straight leg style effectively emphasizing the living curvature of the body, in the round. Seamour turned, smoothly, bending down to pick up our empty water bottle.

Tabitha's calico dress brushing across my thighs with a sigh.

 It never happened.

6. awkward

But it had. And it can be described as much as a medical incident from an anthropological study in a scholarly journal, as it can as a lustful making of love dripping through the pages of some romance novella.

All can be treated with awkward heavy handedness, or with Godly grace. A spanking, or the tickle of a sneeze.

...On this early day of the Spring season, both members of a species fitted together corresponding reproductive systems, fully completing the act of intercourse. Each participant survived the brief encounter, separating amicably.

Some species eat mates after ejaculation, fyi.

But you knew that.

Nah, what is unknown is exactly how it happened. And for this the subtle matter.

The look, the touch.

Little signals that lead up to a tacit yes, come close, as close as possible, to self, to life...

To death.

I can't say what Seamour saw.

We had the evening sun, and I must have been mostly silhouette. The light was catching in our hair, someone might quip it was dreamcatcher like... loose strands in a spider web that should have alerted wayward flies.

What I saw was the Life under the skin, the blush, the rosy lips, as we talked and doubted-over important bits of essentially nothing. A struggle with living... Being. And awareness of that utter futility. An attractive intelligence communicating between us.

Two people.

I would argue, in that moment, two right people.

At that moment.

Destiny conspires, as if, to bring together that which should be cordoned, but for whatever reason is fatally introduced.

Fatally, meaning, life-changing-ly.

Permanently.

Not always.

Just more often, than not, permanently life changing. If not known immediately, then very soon after.

I had taken back the clear bottle.

Seamour's touch holding on a fraction too long. The eyes a pulsating reflection of the sky and trees. Like the Mediterranean Sea. Adriatic. I watched the back of the hand brush across the dampness of lips, a lively unpretentious red, and all the color within the face struck me. Like a painting. Captivating.

I think I thought it *beautiful*. No, not it. Us.

I was suddenly aware of being part of a landscape, everything a work of art, densely woven together so that perception of space was questionable. Every thing was touching everything. Air was not taken for granted as empty space. It was pressing in on us with a warm soft breath.

We'd already sat close. Very close. Too close. The proximity suddenly palpable. I reached out a hand spontaneously and did the unthinkable. Cradling the face. That face. That face that pressed on my heart. My thumb catching one last wayward drop.

"Sorry, I—" almost inaudibly, "I'm so sorry."

The touch turning into caress in mid-sentence and then… us… pulled into fingers that were no longer mine… like ship to anchor at port… blinking a wetness beneath the lashes… grief and relief, wiped with slightest forefinger… withheld waves of emotion, all alike to one or another, each of us as if saved from drowning, now holding on with mouth, with arms and legs, with need… Intensely, holding on for salvation through sudden storm.

Together.

A thing neither of us had been through.

We became a knot.

We had already exchanged so much so that there was a heightened unknown of where one ended and the other began. There were limbs, stroked, and kissed. None of these superfluous. It was necessary, and vital. As in Life affirming. In moments like these, doubtlessly everyone has some awareness of its specialness. A sort of selection, and improbability.

Like in the game aptly named Craps— a roll of dice— and if we feel we are winning, or feel we are losing, we say the same thing: Shit!

Holding Tabitha, that is what I felt.

A deep pause. Because what had we done? Would it change things? Open rifts. Burden each of us, individually, with what we'd tried hard to avoid: Convention. And maybe that very momentary panic was part of that societal conventionality. I held Seamour to my chest and held back a strong impulse to cry out. As if for some loss, unknown.

We see ourself first reflected back in a puddle.

I thought about Narcissus.

In the moment, I wondered, did Seamour have the impression of... I mean, I saw my old haircut... I was stripping my own clothes. But the body was not mine. And in the precise instant, my body was not mine, either. My long hair locked in Seamour's fingers, the small seashell of an ear grazing lightly across my mouth, till we had simultaneously climaxed. For that moment, we each had what the other had.

Or at least, we had "the illusion of."

Conversely, it's a cold imposing observation that masturbation is essentially a homoerotic act.

And then it was over.

Just the throb of the after fuck.

7. reconciliation

Camp. I wondered if that is short for something. Encampment is a military term, isn't it? Or maybe it signifies the age of Fire, when nomads began to live in less hospitable areas and burned meat to break the cellular structure down, to make it chewable.

The Not Paradise.

At least the p isn't silent.

Not like the K in know. Or the p in pneumatic. It was Pneumonia that killed Dad in the final days, compounding all that was already known to be ill. I think P must be the most despised letter. The 16th letter of the alphabet. The 12th consonant. Like Judas? The voiced or unvoiced bilabial stop. Participant in digraphs ph /f/, ps /s/ and pt /t/.

A character symbolizing experience and authority, influence and wisdom.

Power.

Padre.

Like Pope.

Seamour took me to Church one cold pale Spring.

They'd just gotten a new Priest. Irish. Young. Really young. Like what do you call it if it were a woman? Nubile. Tabitha thought it was good. That's what Caufield said.

It shocked us all, though, when the twenty-some-thing-year-old Priest grabbed that giant glass Elephant in the room by the tusk and said:

"When I went to Seminary, my childhood friends said to me, 'Anthony, but why?' ... [the Pastor had a keen dry sense humor, and smiled preemptively, gesticulating pensively. Slowly articulating with accent]... 'Look, man, if it's that you can't find a girl, we'll help you.' [Goodly wait time, for effect. Raising a hand for quiet pause.] ...'Surely, we'll set you up soon with someone. We'll give you some pointers, if you need, pal. Things take time, patience, persistence.'

Wait, I said. No. That's not it, at all.

I've found God.

And having found God, or rather, humbly, please understand [placing a hand on the heart] the Call to serve in vocation, I did not want to exchange that for any worldly thing, or being. I would like you also to know, or to try to recognize as well, that I did not run to the monastery to escape from the world or its problems. Neither on an individual, nor global level. It was not to avoid the rat race, though that [said with a wink] has been a blessing. [Nervous tension released again, as laughter from the general congregation.]

The long and short, is that I am focused on God, and on God's people.

I am here to serve all."

[Heartfelt applause.]

Camp was a lot about competition.

There were races. Scavenger hunts. Cook-offs. And the very evident "invisible" social contest. I want to say Seamour and I were beyond the reach of that. But apparently, environment can sucker you in.

In that brief wretched fifth-grade incident, blinded by admittedly childish hurt and ire, I saw us, Tabitha and I, as EX friends. Any falling out seems dire-in-the-moment. It's like we draft up unwritten bounds, and then who knows if they're breaking them or not?

Those expectations, I mean.

I've learned in the meanwhile to let go of my expectation of others. To give grace. Without arrogance. We can note that it's abusers that have the delusion of controlling others.

Expectation's something you set for yourself.

And keep.

Seamour was as if oppressed by Expectations that Holdan held. Tabitha was to write something, design something, or film some Thing. Something Big. Socially Significant.

"Is that something Holdan wants," I asked, "Or something you *think* is wanted of you? ...Or that You really want?"

"I don't know."

Circled D. All of the Above.

When we were at Camp, we had an argument. Well, not exactly spoken.

As an aside, Holdan had nearly refused to let Tabitha go. Whatever the rationale, only-child attachment, distant fear of molestation, or what, it was nothing compared to the disapprobation my Dad gave. Apparently, the whole Camp was a ploy of social engineering to instill a rift between parents and offspring, taking these younglings out of their nest, as if, before family readiness. A kind of "soft" nanny, or good cop bad cop thing, with who knows what going on as indoctrination.

Seamour and I were ambivalent about it. Going through it together was the thing that mattered.

In any case, we went.

Three "days" of camp, two overnights. And we didn't speak to each other for two days.

On the next morning, after everyone settled in, having set up bunker in customary segregated cabins, boys to the East, girls to the West, the Camp Counselors announced the major Survival Challenge:

"Alright Campers! You'll have your skills tested. Will you make it in the woods? Get lost? Be injured, or lose your lives? ...you'll have this map to share with one team member. This is no ordinary map, you'll have to decipher its riddles. Are you ready?!?!

Alrightie then Campers! On a count of three you'll grab a partner, and it should be I stress Should Be someone you don't know well and girls with girls, boys with boys is strongly suggested. Remember this is Survival!! And anyone without a partner on a count of ten will be partnered at random by Mr. Cregg... So, here we go, look around, look around! Winners of the Survival will get $500 in school bucks. That's right! You heard me. Now here's the countdown. One...Two..."

School bucks incidentally is this phony money that can only be spent at the school store. On erasers, key chains, and that sort of bauble.

I can't exactly pinpoint it. I mean there was no real rational reason. Who the devil would follow some absurd stupid directive in how we should pair up. Like, for, why? Not Tabitha.

Ok, I was livid.

I watched Seamour whisked away by Stephanie. Steph. I could not understand it. My jaw dropped, watching eye to eye as my partner diminished ant-sized. Stephanie gave me a slick lipstick gilded smile. A sixth grader with lipstick looks stupid, never mind a fifth grader. Is that just my opinion? Bracelets jangled and cutesy little flipflops clicked on the camp gymnasium floor. I bet Stephanie thought everything looked really good, from front to back, from the short shorts to the halter top exposing naval bull ring.

I tapped Kaleb, who'd stood next to us.

Oddly, I'm going to admit, I'd had a vagrant toddler crush on Kaleb's Mom. For looks. We saw them, together, in passing. Pick-ups, drop-offs. Something like the awe felt when you see something walk off a page or screen. Mrs. C. looked like a shop window plastic mannikin. Not slutty. Clean, airbrushed, and though flesh and blood, absolutely unattainable. Thanks god. That is important. Because if there were any possibility, the whole infatuation would crash. It had to be pure— the polished look, pretty scent, the sweet sound of whatever casual niceties exchanged, the smooth movement along ordinary daily tasks, the occasional gentle hug hello or goodbye on our play dates— personally, impersonal. Separated in every respect. Anything, otherwise, and the Angelesque would be reduced to shit. You don't go and tarnish the silver you mentally polish.

I only *almost* imagined we kissed.

I liked Kaleb. Tabitha did too. Kale had lived on our street for several years now, and had gone along on a few excursions with us, as unpretentious, inventive, and skilled conversationally.

But inside, I felt betrayed. I was angry. I didn't take it out on anyone, though.

Don't get me wrong.

On that dreaded word of "friends," we had our own and some in common. But when it came to doing things together, for me at least, Tabitha always came first. For years now. Seamour. I guess I didn't much care for God and all God's people. I mean I do, but...

See. I was very particular. I imagine, as an only child (we both were) with no cousins or near-age blood, it was the closest thing to me as having a sibling. To recognize that one person in the crowd anywhere— and my whole face lifted.

I know from the outside.

A stranger once pointed it out to me.

I was waiting at the local Meet N' Greet deli, babysitting an empty Styrofoam cup. Gone cold. Seamour was late and I was getting anxious. Then I hear them! I heard those light quick familiar footsteps, and my heart leapt like some dog from its fireside.

And that family figure surfaced within view...

Seen from the back. Seamour waving goodbye to Holdan. Warmly.

I know it's not all that uncommon.

The expression is absolutely cliché.

"Well, now, I've never seen a face light up like that," said the lady behind the counter, grinning all foxglovelike and wiping invisible crumbs from the Formica nearest my seating.

I remember sharing a glimmer, a glimmer, of my relief over the countertop. The rest I shined on Seamour, who beamed right back, and settled into the swivel stool with notebook in hand and quick reassurances that everything was alright.

8. doubt

My father was ill.

Deathly ill, and Seamour was the only person really who knew. Eventually. Well after.

About Tabitha, Dad had said simply, with a smile and a judicious nod of the head:

"It's good to have someone like that."

Admittedly, I pondered over the "like that." And while I don't think gender was the only thing, it was a considerable part of the "like that." I mean, Dad scoffed at "girlfriend," "boyfriend," as much as either of us. Not that we made anyone privy to the rest of our deliberations. Or, that we didn't talk about it together. We did. Dad and I. Relations.

I scorn the cultural emphasis of Relationships.

People are always worrying over "relationships," in or out or in between. So far as I can see, there is nothing but Relationship. So much so that the term ought to be obsolete. We are in deep, if only with ourselves. I would argue that if you have to "work on it," like extra, you're not really living or something because that is the activity of the brain.

Not on a conscious level.

As a constant. The work in progress.

You and your relationship.

.

Kind of like that dot on the i.

That's the expression we use, isn't it, dotting your i's and crossing your t's... not just a check for details, but a sense of finality. That which never comes until death.

Your final signature.

X

Dad and I weren't really close early on, but we reconnected as if when Mom left. I mean when we found ourselves moving from temporary housing situations to stability. It was on a different plane. We were friends, with all the confidence entailed. It was understood that no one was to know of the sickness we were battling. And when it was clear that it was a losing battle, no one was to know that death was imminent.

Not even Tabitha.

This maybe precipitated the hiccups in our closeness. When you don't want someone to know something, or be affected, you pull away. Maybe it pulled Dad and I closer... I started finding excuses for Seamour not to come over. If we met it was when Holdan was home or at School groups or other busy public places.

We didn't go to my house.

I took up a small menial job to account more for my "unavailability," rather than any other reason. Maybe, also a bit to bolster Dad's perception of my future. That I would make it on my own and be self-reliant. Not that there was any question, but adding doubt at this point seemed wrong. I wanted to be a comfort. I didn't quite fathom the vast expanse of the shadowless plain.

When you're gone, you're gone.

Thinking, or imagining makes it all the more fact.

I don't think that Dad ever questioned Fatherhood. Interesting, small point, which always had me back of my mind guessing if we were even related, was the notion Dad held that every Father must consciously accept or reject Fatherhood in a way that mothers categorically cannot.

"You understand that, right?"

"Yes, sir."

Not having given birth. The act preceding occurring within a window of opportunity, essentially open to other Opportunists, as it were...

Like once open, Pandora is Open.

Spread.

It conjures up some wicked tribal sacrifice rituals of virgin maidens. And blood. As well as all sorts of contraptions ensuring that there, safekeeping, like chastity belts. It's interesting that cats in heat will mate with multiple partners, and all that DNA contributes to the makeup of the offspring. A mix. I suspect that that fear of contamination hovers, and factually, I don't know if it's true for humans, or cats, even, for that matter.

But I can see, though, how an untainted brood would be preferred. Maybe that's why it's called, disparagingly, a cat litter. Or dog litter.

Dad was a dog person as much as a cat person, and early on we had a big black malamute mix. When the dog was dying, I was very young and could not understand the stick that Dad wedged to prop the jaws open in the convulsion of death.

"To prevent biting the tongue off!"

Then it was obvious. I escaped in shame to the silence of the other room, gripping my chest. I thought you pass away… I'd never seen a fight with Death before. Like a match. Invisible and fixed. Giving birth is a similar struggle I imagine. You, out of control of your body, trying to negotiate the pain, the shock, till the spirit that has taken over is released.

See what I mean?

Everything a relationship with Life (you) and Death. (Not you, not I.) Seamour really brought that home.

It occurred to me that without the given additional element of consideration (*the responsibility that came along), Tabitha and I would have gone so far as to make a somewhat different pact.

It would have gone something like this.

Seamour: *Do you feel outa place in this world?*

Me: *I dunno. Not at the moment. But yes.*

Seamour: *Would anyone miss you if we were gone?*

No. If "we," then no.

Me: *We'd go together.*

Tabitha: *You mean that?*

Yes.

It was telling that that was the one thing we didn't talk much about. Death.

We were standing on a bridge, looking down from the edge when I'd had this imaginary conversation with them.

Holdan had a business trip.

Something out in Sacramento, but Tabitha wanted to see the Golden Gate Bridge. Walk along it, I mean. It's about 1.7 miles across, suspension, over 700 feet up. If you've never seen it, the Golden Gate bridge is red brown. Stark, raw. It's something like the hue of traditional Chinese temples coated with Tihong, lacquer pigmented with Cinnabar, red mercuric sulfide. For the bridge paint, architects had picked a very Zen color labeled, "Illuminating Orange."

Later, changed to "International Orange."

It was a glorious evening. Clear, and I was expecting the landmark to shine like the inner workings of a clock mechanism. Golden, and even more so, in the late evening sun. Instead, the bridge was scrawny, dry blood colored. It looked like a stretched-thin caricature of extraterrestrial innards.

We were eleven. I didn't know the name for what I'd meant, inside or out. I drew a blank, except for the concept. Fundamental. And the lack. Its void.

"A birth canal," I whispered.

Tabitha nodded, also verbally blank, else they would have pegged it, as later Seamour was apt to do, precisely and explicitly, as vulva and vagina.

Holdan was also lost. As in, not at all on the same wave:

"The Golden Gate bridge was intended by design to be a golden brown. What happened was that the steel beams that arrived were primed."

We blinked, all the more blank.

"Primed means the steel was pre-painted to protect the material, and ready it for next, and final coating. The beams arrived primed red. That made it futile to paint them light. The architects picked an orange red, and insisted it was better. They argued it is more visible for boat and air traffic."

"Why didn't they change the name?"

"Well, the color itself didn't actually matter," said Holdan.

"You mean they didn't name the bridge for what it looks like?"

"Nope."

"Then I don't get it," I said.

Holdan looked at us children for a moment with pursed lips. The way a professor must look when about to make an important edifying remark:

"It's named rather for the water that runs below it. The Strait."

"What?" I knew Seamour was thinking, wait, the water isn't golden either. It's Pacific turquoise, a clear warm blue-green. But then I thought maybe it's the way the sunsets... colorized Goldwyn Hollywood.

"Chrysopylae," Holdan continued. "Meaning, Golden Gates. The Strait was likened to the Golden Horn of Byzantium. During the Gold Rush it was the passageway for commerce, said to be: *'A golden gate to trade with the Orient...'!*"

So, it all came down to the buck.

Holdan laughed, as the wind kicked up sending Tabitha's locks flowing forward towards the water, like a Siren. Pulling home.

"Actually, they were going to paint the bridge yellow and black, in broad vertical stripes."

"Like a bumble bee?"

Holdan gave a silent No, and grimaced:

"Like a construction sign."

"...like a crime scene," Seamour said taking my hand, and moving us on. The turning hair catching my face. A definite chill settled in on dimming of the light. Crossing the bridge, we heard someone, in long dark trench and fedora, playing Auld Lang Syne on harmonica, well behind us.

My extended fascination with Robert Burns begs explanation. And, I guess, it all comes down to circumference of the skull. Some things take on cult like significance. Larger than life. After thirty-eight years of burial, the body was exhumed so cranial measurement could be made.

For the size of Genius. Universality.

"Why not Frost?" asked Tabitha, as a child. Holdan didn't have an answer. But I understood, for Holdan it was an air of nostalgia, for how we simplify. It had nothing to do with the poet. I've misheard lyrics enough awful times to feel the density of recognition. Ugh! saying to myself, "How could a person (or, I) be so mistaken?!" Because the "corrected" version often loses something on revision, and I know that loss. Holdan shrugged at the history, putting emphasis on the effect of the poetry:

"It sounded right. At the time."

It continued to intrigue me, as much as it put Seamour off. Too much emphasis. Holdan had given Tabitha a giant tome of collected songs and poems by Robert Burns, as well as an old vinyl. And eventually, Seamour let me have these.

Burns had dropped the e in the old surname, had scrambled 'round in various occupations, and implicated dames in a family way, till finally getting comfortable as a writer. A poor man who "made it." As a professional author.

They say Burns was pre-cursor to the Romantics.

"Comin' Thro' the Rye" had its start as a poem, written in 1782, but then the original Burns lyrics mutated in song. And it wasn't that nobody caught anybody. They didn't *save* them, across the abyss.

They *were* caught. As in caught up.

Seems the lad and lassie did a jig, over time, and in reversal, lost any name at all, in verse. What they had left, hanging then was this overwhelming sense of ambiguity, coming through, with hints of shame, and longing.

Ambiguity was complete. Thorough, in person and place. And despite the Scottish language briers, a commonality prevailed.

The Rye might well be a field, a street, or the grass adjacent to some waterfront.

To the tune of the Scottish Minstrel, "Common' Frae the Town" ...incidentally, same as Robert Burns chose for the lyrics to Auld Lang Syne... a crooner would now sing in edit:

If a body meet a body
Comin' thro' the rye,
Coming through the rye
If a body kiss a body need a body cry?
Ev'ry laddie has his lassie
None, they say, have I
Yet all the lassies smile on me
When comin' thro' the rye.
If a body meet a body
Comin' from the town
If a body greet a body
Need a body frown?
Ev'ry laddie has his lassie
None, they say, have I

Yet all the lassies smile on me
When comin' thro' the rye.
Upon the train there is a swain I dearly love myself
But what's her name or where's her name I do not
choose to tell
Ev'ry laddie has his lassie
None, they say, have I
Yet all the lassies smile on me
When comin' thro' the rye.

What happened to the wet petticoat? Or what's 'er name? ... I see us as lost. All of us.

Gone missing.

And each, missing each other, out there.

Like "Jenny."

9. Alone

It was summer. I had told no one.

I was found out.

I simply hadn't thought about how bills come due. It was a seemingly small thing. Easy to omit, in distress. Of course Dad had set certain things into motion for me, having great foresight, despite the duress. I mean, the bills were long since put on auto-pay, the bank account specially selected as combined Savings and Checking. Some sort of annuities or bonds or something poured in on a regular basis and it covered no frills living. Housing, utilities, and frugally, I could draw from it for food and household goods with debit card. Dad had a thing for discipline and independence and passed it to me.

And I still had my little bakery line job.

What we didn't figure was the dog.

They took Irving first.

Our Pitbull mix, a bitch with a howl so eerie it was a ghost story in itself. I still remember that sound, as the dog catcher's van drove out with a cloud of dust from our neighborhood.

Knock, knock.

Of course I didn't answer. I peered out through the curtain. I saw a white dark-window sedan. Parked a ways away. Just beyond the driveway entrance. Still visible to me from up here despite the tangle of small trees and the smattering of leaves.

The clip of heels alerted my ears that there's something like a town official on the stoop. And I detected an additional set of feet, creeping. Someone had gone around the grassy back. Irving barked. That wretched pitiful yelp that Pitbulls have, almost discrediting their fearsome bite.

Then a flat voice:

"They still have it."

I found the notice in the mailbox when they left. A seemingly no big deal:

Dog license expired. Owner will renew in person. Remit late fee within one week. City Hall M-F 9-5.

Except it was.

Town regulations stipulating that a person must be at least 18 years of age to own a dog.

I suppose if I'd taken Seamour into confidence ...if I'd been honest with Holdan... a lot of grief might have been spared. Like maybe the two of them would have co-opted me into their household accounting. What's five or six years or so? Till college. Of course, at that point I didn't know I *had* a scholarship coming and enough state aid to help me work my way through. To actually go.

But if it could have been "Holdan's dog" on paper, then maybe I'd have continued to live at 104 Brook Avenue with Irving. Right. By myself. Maybe.

The trouble was in the persistence of the local bureaucratic machine. I'd no idea. Apparently that 28 odd bucks was an important part of the town economy. It was when the police came that I finally unlatched the door.

They already declared they were entering, with or without my opening...

Funny thing was Dad's cremation was simple. Two men came in to take the body, on my calling the designated phone number.

"Hello, which room?" said the taller of the two men. Both dressed in scrubs, dark mechanic like, but still scrubs. I pointed over to the living room and they shuffled single-file conversing amongst themselves on some lingering flow.

"And the smell! Mhph!"

"Really??! Huh. Grilled tuna with mushrooms and parmesan, goodness who would have thought!"

"So good. On the grill. You gotta try it."

I caught the second guy's eye with a disconcerted look of self-reassessment and vague reproach. I told them quite unnecessarily that my apparently absent Mom was just too distraught to meet them, then they were brusquely understanding, carrying on in their task with appropriate silence.

Jostling the weight like fully dead material.

Not a person.

Picking up the ashes was also impersonal.

The service rendered was prepaid according to Dad's arrangement and premortem signatures. The ashes were sent back home, meaning to me, via USPS. A small surprisingly heavy box. I didn't even need to sign for it.

No one had been aware that I was alone.

Until Animal Control had the Police pound on my door. They administratively waited out my lies, and when I couldn't give a proper contact number or address for kin or legal guardian within allotted business hours, they took Irving to the pound.

They said they'd be back. To get me.

If no one showed up.

And no one did.

Till State Police troopers brought Child Protection Services in...

I was watching Kwik.tv and drinking water. We didn't have to pay for it then in that neighborhood. Water. Well water is what we had. That always seemed to impress other folks when Dad would mention it.

Well water. Like it meant exactly what it said.

For me it was one less expense.

Fact was the town had had a radium scare. It had been in the papers and then quickly quelched. Underground. It had to do with land use. Or misuse. The council was seeking to stop-gap some hemorrhaging of uncollected tax dollars from failed small businesses, as well as gauged residents who could no longer afford to pay for their house and property (and in a bust market opted to abandon ship). And so, the town was selling out to commercial development. Quick. Like for some road or water channel, or dump...

And we were warned not to drink the water.

In one of these buyout schemes, land had been designated as a commercial hazardous waste site. Burial. The containers were cheap, of course.

They leaked.

I had the conscientious anxiety that I had money to live on, just wasn't sure how much or for how long, and stopped buying bottled. I wanted to get through school. I was sitting on the fading black velour couch contemplating the what next.

Frugally.

Sipping that tap.

Irving! we'd likely never see each other again. I was sitting, thinking foolishly— maybe I should go to the pound. You know, check. Absurd as it was. I could do nothing or nothing that seemed rational. Break in? Fake an id? Beg or bribe a stranger?

Irving was christened immediately when Dad and I visited a family friend's place. We had no stated intentions actually of getting a dog. At the time, in particular. I mean, sure maybe, someday. Then, in a corner of that kitchen, in a plain large cardboard box with some towels, we saw three pups. Free to good home.

One with no head.

That's the body I picked up and the paws released, revealing a well tucked, very cute, wrinkled, and slobbering face. I was nine and grasped the tan wiggler with as firm a hand as I could— turning this way and that from the wet puppy nose and tongue that also emerged instantaneously from nowhere.

"Legend of Sleepy Hollow," Dad laughed.

"Washington Irving," I said.

And it stuck.

"Wait. Irving? Like 'The World According to Garp'?" Tabitha asked incredulously several years later when they made us read it as avant-garde risqué prescribed reading material.

I shook my head.

Odd how things would seem to intertwine. I half-assed my reading of the book. The High School teacher lost me at the word Feminism. Maybe I should revisit.

Seamour read it. Thorough.

In any case, once again, I became a ward of the State. It was a period of about 10 months before I got placed. A full human gestation. I didn't realize that then— Everyone says "nine months," but it's 40 weeks.

It was that time in fostering that Seamour and I began making our swaps. Incrementally.

By the month Mom showed up, my hair was shoulder length. My body, soft, whittling into a thin string.

Life would harden me soon enough.

"Honey I..."

I guess things moved forward quickly for Mom.

A long trail of ellipses trailed. The dot on that i so fragmented and far off that we could both feel its loss of gravity.

Worse.

There was that grin, like when you don't know what to say and are experiencing some delight in deluded judgement, having won some silent argument. Satisfaction at the resultant situation of someone else, as reflecting somehow in your favor. Superiority or inferiority.

A smile down, it should be called.

Mom had it worked out so the lawyers would make the case for foster care without too much of a negative reflection on parental character. The case was even easier to make on seeing the despondent charge.

No contest.

"They?" Mom said, mouth still twitching with errant pleasure. It was not a pertinent matter after all, was it. Mom adjusted the nice clothes picked specially for this appearance. Mostly jewelry.

I shrugged cooly: "Yeah, you left us."

That wiped the smile, and the subsequent flash of anger was replaced with stiff composure. I was somebody else's problem. It would be official. The forms were signed.

I didn't tell Mom it was Jenny now.

The case worker left. I was in the room alone a moment, and figured I was "live." On some hidden camera monitor.

Or maybe nobody gave a shit.

I sat waiting for the temporary foster family.

I am going to say, perhaps defensively, or pre-emptively, that whatever we did, you and I, we didn't do it for show. And I know that seems strange, because so much of it revolves around the visual.

We swapped our hairdos. We exchanged wardrobes, right down to our underwear, for chrissake.

But I don't blame our parents.

We weren't mad. At anyone in particular.

10. Prego

I had a strange gestation.

Knowing my life would change. The situation was almost comical because I could see myself in the position of an oversized fetus. I was sort of inside/outside of "the womb" simultaneously. Ignorant of outcome and conscious, oddly, having advantage of prior experience.

"You'll be born again," Seamour said wryly.

I wasn't a blank slate, though.

I knew I should have a Mom and a Dad. A domicile. These were known unknowns. I knew my name. Given and selected. I guess I even knew who I was. In character. Known, knowns. My height, I was pretty sure would be about what it was. Average.

I mean, I could change a lot. If I wanted. Yet.

I felt I was cognizant through and through. I could dye my hair, and still know the real color. Contacts could change how I looked to you, but everything would be with the same bias, looking from the inside, out. I could put wolf's skin on, or sheep's.

Underneath it all, the infant would be me.

And I wailed, silently, inside. I wanted to go Home. In all the ambiguity that entails. I was mourning some past existence I thought was mine...

Familiarity... how we love that Devil from birth!

It occurred to me, as well, in the moment, that I could even go ahead and change sex. Not that I thought to actually go that far, though. I remember in one of our last years of middle school, Sean had been bouncing off the wall. The whole chose-your-own-gender thing just boggled the mind. At the time, Sean was modestly religious (actually, claiming to be Buddhist). When talking, though, I'd say a definite Christian upbringing showed through. I mean, in the personification of God.

Anyway, Sean says suddenly, why if God gives you one set of junk, is it ok for a person to cut something out, or add something in?

We were all gathered between classes at the end of the hall and one of the teachers (not mine) was hanging with a bunch of us and entertaining Sean's questions. What Mr. Devrie pointed out was that Sean, and Elijah who was also standing among us, both had "in essence," body modification, if not exactly, mutilation.

It took a minute to center on a word.

No one assembled had any pulled earlobes, or piercings, or colored plastic decor embedded in the skin, or anything drastic. Devrie was pointing to their body art. A red and green tribal design ran down Sean's mocha right arm, and thin black geometric patterns extended onto Elijah's right hand.

"It's a tattoo." Sean said like Devrie didn't know.

Devrie was almost as animated as Sean, saying: "Augmentation is augmentation," and "...Body dysmorphia is a thing!"

I don't think most of us knew what that was. And I'm not sure what the point was, exactly.

"Yeah, well you can *remove* a tattoo," Elijah speculated.

"I don't know if you can, or can't, do-over *that* operation, but I just don't get how you can think you're a girl, if you see you're a boy!?!" said Sean, bouncing from the wall, both hands gesticulating. One hand was holding a bristle brush. For hair.

"That's the thing," said Devrie. "They don't see."

That's what dropped the jaw for us. Like, whoa, I understood what schizophrenia is... I think most of us did.

"Wait," I said.

Sean started brushing again, and leaned back comfortably, to listen.

"Are you suggesting people who get a sex change have something like... mental illness?"

"Well..." a tacit yes flowed from the eyes.

The very thought overwhelmed us. I mean if you don't see what "everybody" else sees, it IS considered being delusional, isn't it?

"What about anorexics?" said Devrie, as if in negation, reading the scene.

I shifted uncomfortably.

"What about them?" Sean shrugged.

"You are all up in alms," Devrie said looking at Sean, like at a bigot, "just because it's the idea of a man changing to a woman. There's vice versa, you know! Women who wake up feeling like men, too, and go through with the whole operation!!"

"I know, but I'm a MAN!" Sean said.

"Well, you don't have to sleep with them!" Devrie exclaimed as if excavating some secret underlying dark psychological dilemma for Sean and punctuating the conversation with a raised index finger.

But it was only the bell that rang with any certainty.

"How would we even know…" Deontay whispered low, as we dispersed.

I knew I wasn't a candidate.

My thoughts after this exchange were filled with elevated empathy for anyone who would go so far as to have that procedure done. I felt they must be quite far gone, psychologically. Call it conviction, or fanaticism, faith, or disease.

It was commitment.

I told Seamour about it later. Well later. It arose because I recalled that Elijah had kept bringing up something about monkeys and evolution, in the same conversation, repeatedly asking Devrie, "if THIS is what God wants?" I inferred that the question concerned neutralization of gender.

It popped into my head when reading, "On The Origin of Species," for some school paper I was drafting out.

"Hey, looks like here's the part where they carved out "Survival-of-the-Fittest,'" I said marking the passage with highlighter: "*It is not the strongest of the species that survive, nor the most intelligent, but the one most responsive to change.*"

"Yes," Seamour answered enigmatically, "process of elimination," taking up the volume from me.

I knew that since forever, Tabitha was thorough, and purposeful. They'd read this before, I could tell as they turned deliberately to another part to read aloud very slowly:

"Man selects only for his own good; Nature only for that—"

"wait, huh, no...?! like that would put mankind "outside" of Nature? I mean, well, doesn't Nature select...?" like first, or foremost...

"Point made," said Seamour closing the book and handing it back. I wondered about oversight or lack thereof. Right. That had been after all Elijah's concern: that "Someone" would "will" things this way. Because the idea that it would just "happen" seemed irresponsible... out of control.

Or maybe just outside of human construct.

I pushed a yellow index card across the table with another quote: *"We are always slow in admitting any great change of which we do not see the intermediate steps"*— Charles Darwin.

Seamour nodded in acknowledgement.

Devrie had latched onto the seemingly pejorative mention of monkeys. That Elijah and others didn't want to be "associated." As if dissing evolution.

"You know, a lot of animals are wayyyyyy more intelligent and sophisticated than humans are," was what Devrie had said.

Sean balked in opposition, that animals can't talk. Or read, or write, or draw.

"That's kinda frivolous to survival," I said.

"Art?!"

Admittedly, aghast, I felt disloyal to myself for a moment. Actually, I was surprised. Impressed, even, that it seemed at all that important to Sean, or anyone, really, anymore.

Devrie spoke then animatedly and eloquently, describing the nonverbal and unexamined communication of dolphins, rats, and bees... All received, skeptically.

It was a good point.

"Sean," I said, "When we talk, we have to be within a few feet of each other, just as far as we can shout. Else we need a crutch to lean on. A device," I added, holding up someone's wayward cell for illustration.

A moment of pause.

I'd read about those test animal experiments where lab rats were given various puzzles to solve. It was as if one problem solver rat, after a bit of struggle, immediately passed along the know-how to all the other lab rats. The task no longer a challenge.

We don't do that. Telepathically, I mean. It gets hidden in words. In books. In devices. In code.

*

It takes time.

I should have known.

Older children don't get adopted easily.

I'd heard that again and again, and braced myself for something of a nomadic life, of being pushed from one host home to another, before my fate was "formalized." I wondered why somebody should adopt me. It was a question as much about my own characteristics, as those of the adoptees.

Would I be designated as hands for domestic labor? I was big enough, strong, quick witted and capable. I figured that would be easily seen and advertised. As advantage. Maybe I'd be billed as a consolation for some childless couple? I was polite and unassuming enough, I guess. Or maybe I'd make a fine pet for lonely empty nesters? I imagined some arbitrary trait might tickle the fancy, a cowlick or a freckle, and they would dote on me for no particular reason, except to reinforce the time old notion that childhood and indulgence are somehow synonymous. Nostalgically, like, among family households not warped by mental instability or substance abuse.

It's unknown unknowns that really get to you.

For all my imaginings, I failed to picture what actually happened.

I got adopted.

Eventually.

It's called a pregnant pause when somebody knows something you don't yet and it's about to drop.

I had also, more cynically, thought about those who take in kids to get that little stipend that comes with. Plus, those modest perks that can add up. Like Head of Household tax status and EIC (Earned Income Credit) or Exemptions for dependents. Food stamps.

I knew about all that pragmatically from Dad. And I'm not judging folk. Reasons vary.

After the quickly convened court hearing, in which Irving's "well-being" was discussed before mine, I was taken to what's called a group home. Same day service, which told me the governmental machinery was duly organized. Orphanages are considered passé, as an "institution." Nowadays. But really, a building where parentless children are made to go on local government stipend, is still a ward full of lost and homeless youth.

AKA Orphans.

When the Judge gave the address, reading aloud the official Court decision in the matter of me vs the State, it was ordered that I would take up residence at 932 Shadybrooke.

All I knew, immediately, was that it wasn't home. The subsequent van ride was long, and I could see it was unfamiliar countryside. And it sounded like an old person's community.

Where people go to die.

Or an asylum.

11. Silence

It was a strange isolation.

I want to write that time off.

Camp hadn't adequately prepared me for being away from home. What it means, when there is no going back. No, that time was something like a religious experience.

Transcending. I had momentarily lost contact with the world, as I knew it. Floating in space, waiting out some indeterminate time in a dark airless incubator. I all but stopped talking beyond what the modicum of courtesy and function would require.

I might as well have mutated into some alien lifeform.

Shadybrooke. The e was silent. Of course, I noted the name of my home street in that "Boulevard," as it turned out to be. There were human characters there, in what I'd more accurately call a Shelter. It was on the far side of town. In a different zoning district.

"Of course, you'll go to your own school," the case worker finally said, clicking a pen, filing some incoming paperwork perfunctorily: "But it won't be at least for a couple days. We've had a hiccup in transportation."

I only wanted to see Seamour.

I knew I had a lot of explaining to do and it was suddenly dawning on me again the damage unaccounted-for silence creates. We make things up. Nature abhors the void. In its stead, vacuum. Suction for the unsaid, the presumed —I suppose I've felt a vacuum my whole life, from the fragmentation of family.

What happened to you? is not a question I've ever been comfortable in breaching. Everyone has a story. Maybe they're not ready to tell it.

"I survived a car crash," Raymond said breaking the sound barriers after we'd sat the next morning pushing some cold cereal in the kitchenette. The host family was okay. I mean they understood that we need space and did all the chauffeuring and basic needs business expediently. Maybe it was evident to the adults that if anybody reached out to talk, never mind touch me, I'd blow a fuse.

Lash out.

But Raymond was our age, and in the same debacle. Somehow the words fell through into my conscious without violence. It was cold in t-shirt and jeans. I wished I'd grabbed a jacket— from home.

My shoulders curled in.

"My Dad died," I answered stiffly, and saw in my periphery the tall, thin, nod. Empathetic, like, oh I only had "one," as if that were the greater loss, somehow, than Raymond's both parents, out at once in an accident.

So, I corrected quietly, "My mom's still alive."

Raymond nodded again, with sympathy, the long ski cap bobbing along in accord. As if it was understood also that some kind of sad sickness was involved here. A common cold. Uncurable.

All around.

According to the monitor list on the fridge, there were four of us. The other two were siblings, shadows of each other. Seldom exiting their room.

I wasn't sure how many years a person could stay in this host limbo. It looked like they'd been in for a long time. Ashen. Silent. Like monks.

Day two, in this monochrome, I started to think it might be doable to slide through to adulthood in this sort of anonymity. Even if it meant years.

The Missus of the house stopped me in my stupor:

"They'll be transferring you this afternoon."

Said pleasantly, mildly, without explanation. I wanted to ask whether it was school related or personal or what. A carnival wheel of emotion, thinking maybe I'd get to Seamour? Maybe not. Then, the dread that this is the way it was going to be. A constant shuffle. I calculated the distance from the second-floor window to the trimmed lawn.

I wasn't sure I could make it.

I worked on my posture.

The hosts had two children of their own. Real family people, a boy and a girl, and these were "unreal" in their TV all-American model presence. I guess I'm probably so off center that the median Norm is suddenly distinctly visible.

They weren't attractive. They were just remarkably average, unquestioning, and "well adjusted."

Confident.

Stare worthy.

They had some ordinary things to do. A haircut appointment and ball practice. The older one grabbed the car keys, and they drove off. Waving to Mom and Dad. I watched those jangling car keys, like an animal, mesmerized. In the movements I identified with something. Tick, tock, tick, tock. I could even name it at once. That, that could be me—

independent.

And I know that should have a capital i.

We're all still chasing that dot.

Yeah, I felt like a locked-up cat. Ready to climb the screen doors. I thought to ask to use the phone. The thought, futile. They'd say yes, I was sure of it.

Stupidly I didn't have the number.

The foretold switch-of-housing was a block out from my own neighborhood. Like, who knew these "host homes" were so near, among us all this time? The boulevard family was clean. Squeaky clean Americana. In the block-away location, it was a different sitcom. There was a beer bellied man-woman of the house and an equally gutted woman-man. A pair of boobs. The differentiation between them cosmetic. If it wasn't for the narrow difference in proportion of makeup and facial hair I'd be fully confused.

Both had medium shaggy hair. One dyed yellow-red, the other purple-green. Between the two of them there wasn't a visible piercing missing. Eyebrow, lip, tongue, nose, cheek, chin and all around the ears. There were no biological children here. Just us add ons, and mixed company at that.

They oogled us all.

"That's a pretty one, heheh," I heard one cracking to the other, and then some chuckling. Even their voices were in a similar range, more or less, eunuched. I had a moment of pause. I might have had sympathy. No, I should have. A sense of solidarity even, in the evident complete disregard for gender modes. But I didn't. I couldn't. There was nothing intellectual here.

No conviction, Seamour would say.

No fight.

It was, if I had to summarize it up, something like resignation. In the way debauchery is a form of resigning oneself to base impulses. Like laziness. Indifference. Ease. While still having to actively meet basic needs.

Physical, emotional.

I had one small bag, a satchel. It was made of leather and had been imported from someplace in Europe. I don't know who in fact had brought it in, by plane. It'd been in our attic for years, deemed too high quality to use. I liked its old-world character and Dad eventually said I could have it. It was perfect for a book and a journal and some drawing pens. Not exactly a travel duffle. I think you'd call it an attaché. I wanted to stay light, and had rolled up a couple of socks, boxers and t-shirts very tightly and lined the bottom. My notebook was on top, and a narrow thermos tucked on one side.

I was getting the impression that there'd be some dull forced socialization around here. I heard heavy foot falls, and the kind of hesitation that occurs just before tapping. I had the window already open, first floor. Low. They'd let the Rottweiler in, I could hear. I raised the screen, shifted the satchel out, and straddled the sill.

Then, I heard someone try the door knob— and leapt.

I ran like hell through the yard. Scaled the chain link, tearing some skin.

Heart pounding. Feet and breath pounding.

The world was darkening out along the edges. But instead of feeling swallowed, or inhaled, by the coming twilight, I felt expelled. It's interesting the whole discussion on freedom. The essential question being: Freedom to, or Freedom from?

I was on side of freedom from, finally.

Seamour had tried to impress it upon me, and I had faltered in understanding:

"You can be free to do a hundred thousand things… but I bet anything, what you really want is freedom from just one."

Suffering.

Yes, all those discomforts, like fear, pain, hunger, and disease. I wanted to be free *from*.

Not just for me.

My pace slowed. I held my heart and listened:

"Gen X," I heard Holdan saying, "..." the voice trailing off into the incandescent living room, so familiar and soul warming. I strained to hear Seamour through the cracked open windows. Then it occurred to me to run around out back to the patio. They watched the sunset there, more often than not, and Holdan wouldn't blink an eye at seeing me.

Nothing known to be amiss.

But Seamour looked awful. The living-dead sitting in the red-purple evening. A flashbulb went off in Tabitha's glance on sighting me. That white bright dot in the eye that painters painstakingly put in—to mimic Life. I put my hand out, not to get up, and squatted down next to the lounge chair. Holdan was still prattling on inside, in a burgundy smoking jacket, fixing some cold drinks on a tray.

Looking all professorial.

"...oh, Jenny, didn't see you come in. Lemonade ok, or Iced Tea?"

"Lemonade, yes, please."

That's what I saw sparkling in the pitcher, against the backlight of the kitchen, with ice and a long thin wooden spoon stuck in. Fresh squeezed.

Holdan handed us each a glass and went back in for a third.

Where the fuck were you hung in the air between us.

"I got picked up by CPS," I said quickly, in a hush. Catching my breath: "Child Protection Services." Suddenly I felt something like a criminal. Wanted. I wondered just how long it would take for legal repercussions.

I could see, for Tabitha, it was a far worse transgression than Camp had been for me. These three long torturous unheard from days.

As a single Dad, Holdan had been very careful to be present. The conversation continued:

"Would you believe that there is no legal age set for leaving a child home alone?"

I had caught at the tail end of the conversation, on entering the backyard, that Gen X was also known as the Latchkey generation.

I'd been left home alone a lot, even since before kindergarten. In retrospect, I think I was grateful for it. At the time not so much. Right now, all I wanted was to be left alone. From strangers. And I could steadily hear a vehicle approaching along the fence. Really, really, slow. Then, footsteps. Authoritative. An over-sized search light right behind, soundlessly found me. The dark figure fully obscured.

I didn't want any trouble for Holdan or Tabitha.

I stood up. I imagined myself in a Western.

I was going to take this like a man, right? I even hammed it up a little, because why not go on out and say all deep:

"You lookin' for me?"

It didn't go as planned. My voice cracked.

But I didn't flinch. I kept walking and didn't do the Lot's wife mistake. I looked straight ahead. It was just a county unmarked car. The driver was my casework, Gunther McAlister.

The other was a County Police Officer.

Outfitted.

Seamour would have to explain it to Holdan—at some point. In the meantime, McAlister started explicating things to me in a whiny protest:

"You can't run off 'n not expect consequences. Now, we go to the courthouse."

"Before the judge?"

"Yes."

I didn't have to ask how they'd found me.

It was still plenty daylight when I'd dropped out the window. And I'd ran like I had a bladder emergency, a couple blocks down, with lots of people who knew me. People who, if asked, wouldn't think twice to point right to Holdan's place. Or mine.

Thinking nothing of it. Helping *me* out.

It's a strange thing the way communication has evolved. They tell little kids all the time: "Use your words." I feel a bit awkward, socially, broaching the subject. People with cognitive delays and physical limitations have been hidden away less and less over the years.

We took note of the disabled more in high school. Everyone started talking about Gen Ed (as opposed to Special Ed) about inclusion, and educational integration, developmentally.

Some individuals I noticed had little binders on straps filled with small icons. These read Yes or No. Some had pictures as well, like a frown with No and a smile with Yes, a picture of a juice box for

Drink, a picture of a lunch tray with food for Hungry.

Some had sturdy plastic computer tablets.

They call these devices.

And the directive is still, "use your words."

Some devices are smaller. Discreet. We call these cellphones. Everyone using their words.

More or less.

Text.

It got me thinking about ASD characteristics. Specifically, the common trait that people on-the-spectrum don't speak much, if at all. But they have other ways of communicating.

Like words on some surface.

Just a note.

I didn't have a phone myself actually until after I was adopted. And then it was understood to be vital for emergency contact. Sarah gave it to me quickly:

"Everyone should have one."

.

In ten months, I was taken in by two moms.

"To spite your Mother," Seamour said, aptly.

It wasn't all what you'd think. Maybe it was, maybe it wasn't, this is how it unfolded for me.

Elizabeth and Sarah Perkins.

Two ladies, pushing well on into their sixties, I guessed. Spinsters, I was told, and sisters. Hence, the commonality of the surname. At this point I was no stranger to lurid insinuation. I had every right, so it seemed, to be alert to potential threats to my person, even if directly they might have nothing to do with me. Which is how it occurred to me that they might closetedly be incestuous lesbians.

And then, the humane secondary reflection:

What of it?

If it had nothing to do with me, and no violence or force was involved with any other person, then it's not a crime between them... Whose business is it, among consenting individuals? I was annoyed with my ugly thinking.

Of course, they were likely entirely innocent.

Imagination is mean. Just two old ladies, sad not to have had any kids of their own— or husbands for that matter. Maybe so sad, as actually never having any lovers, even? That sort of situation must also happen more frequently than anyone would care to admit. Deviating from picturesque norm of "our" shared societal expectations.

That unwritten timeline of what *Everybody* else does, or should, and by when. Social pressure. I can't call it peer pressure.

It comes at you from within.

I don't know, but I guess I took pity on them. You'll observe that I had to adopt them as much as they adopted me. As a teenager, I had this right, legally. By natural order, I had this prerequisite, mentally.

Never mind, emotionally.

Something about my look, I expected, was what might have prompted them to take an interest in me. I imagine I looked like a wiry difficult obstinate child. It was, in any case, something that wasn't easily "overlooked."

They said I'd been in the paper.

"Just done broke my heart, the way you lost your Dad, and then your dog, and your home, and your neighborhood, everything, really," Elizabeth said. "You'd every right to go and lose your head, and go stir crazy, poor thing. I'm sure I would."

Elizabeth was the rotund of the two. Short. White gold puffy shoulder bobbed haired, with thin wire rimmed glasses kept on a sparkling beaded strand, referred to as the lanyard. Quick to smile, sweetly, Elizabeth looked very huggable. Sarah seemed the firmer of the two, with a somewhat hawkish look, like a branch that dried and stiffened while reading under the stars or something. Definite, yet abstract, thoughtful, kind. Salt pepper hair cropped in short eaves, over large pale hazel eyes. I had the funny impression that Elizabeth was ruled by heart and Sarah by reason.

They seemed nice.

"We realize we wouldn't be adopting you for long, maybe, but it just seems like the right thing to do."

Squeezing my hand lightly and then Sarah's, Elizabeth continued: "I feel like God is guiding us in this decision, and it will prove to be a lifelong blessing. Of course, *we* may not live all that long."

They stared at me in earnest. Unison.

"What do you think," Elizabeth didn't yet add "dearie?" but I swear I heard it. I felt like they really didn't have any agenda, together or individually, to change me. Just a genuine compassionate need to help, because they were in that position where they thought that they could. Or should. Help.

They had come to this agreement amongst themselves based on collected case files and newspaper clippings. And something else, I didn't yet fathom.

"We live near your old neighborhood."

"Actually, we're thinking of buying the house. Your house, I mean," Elizabeth beamed.

"If we can close on it," said Sarah.

It occurred to me that I could easily call them Mom. House or no house. It was a beautiful sentiment, even in its abstraction.

I had entirely given up on going "home" home.

"Ok," I sighed and signed. "Let's go."

12. falling Out

"Class, classss?"

"Yes, yes?"

"For thisss project, we'll pick a favorite song, or painting, or other artwork, for inspiration and create something in a Complementary art form. Ok? For example, if you pick a song, it has words, music, but no picture. Ssso, you'll add the visual. If you pick a painting, there is no verbal or auditory. Ssso you might make a story, or a song. We'll work these into a digital classs presentation all together during the week of our final Parent Teacher conferences. Does anyone have any questions, at thisss point?"

Phae showed us some student samples.

"Can we videotape a dance?"

"What if we pick a film?"

I've forgotten to mention that Phae was our homeroom teacher but certified in Language Arts.

And this was an English assignment, in effect, as we would have to write and speak about our thought process, and the resulting work, whatever the media. It was what Phae called our "capstone" project for the year to be completed during our daily WIN period.

If you're not familiar the acronym stands for What I Need, and it happens every day in that strange window before or after lunch, which is really one ordinary class period divided in half. Designated to be used for social emotional learning and enrichment.

That was when Tabitha got a haircut.

Not a trim. Not like a new do, in layers, or something. A shearing, with scissors. A very conspicuous do it yourselfer. It turned out, on presentation day, after much secrecy over the project itself, Seamour had chosen to do some performance art.

I knew the selection of work was Mark Twain's thick book, the "Recollections of Joan of Arc," sometimes published simply as "Joan of Arc."

One Life is all we have and we live it as we believe in living it, Tabitha had quoted.

I thought Seamour would choose to do some drawing or painting. They had some serious skills. Like they could do that up on stage with the whole world watching, and it would be awesome. People would be entranced.

That's not how it went down. It was painful to watch. Which is not to say it wasn't "well done." Or that people weren't fully absorbed in it. In abstraction, you might even say it was brilliant and self-sacrificing.

Tabitha chose to do a mime.

In absolute silence we watched, for the five-minute limit, a rapid pantomime of Joan's life.

I was reminded of other painful watches. Like the installation show of the potato peeler in the MOMA, monotonously peeling in silence, for hours on end. Or the short film on the obsessive raisin counter.

Time stops. And the act replays itself maliciously over and over in your imagination, extending itself further in duration. When not watching.

You are maybe familiar somewhat? Jehanne Darc was an illiterate peasant of Domremy, somewhere in Northeastern France, in 1412, and became patron saint of the country for valor during the

Hundred Years' War, leading demoralized troops to unlikely victory at age 17, and then was burned at the stake at age 19, having been handed over to the English by the French Burgundian traitors, for supposed "heresy." Specifically, for blaspheming, by wearing men's clothes and acting on visions.

Seamour had devised several hand puppets that helped to illustrate the opposing camps. The paper characters hovered in front of the arms, leaving both hands exposed and free to push along the ensuing action. With tools and gestures.

Completely absorbed, I saw Tabitha as Joan d'Arc. The non-reality was dispelled initially by the first wave of emotion that the written description on PowerPoint projector evoked. Horror at the very history. The youth. The faith. The evocativeness of "Visions." The brutality of the death foretold.

Tabitha, acting with left hand as executioner, made it real— chopping off inches of Real hair— trimmed for war, first, and then loped quick to the scalp, preparing for the stake. That did it. The double take. The whole class gasped, and whatever Tabitha had done after or before was effectively subjected to a real disbelief. No longer suspended.

I even heard several "Oh my gods!" fall.

The stake was completely fake—a cardboard pole attached to a foldable stepstool covered in yellow and red tissue paper. It readily waved in the slightest breeze. On climbing up, Seamour let loose dry ice from a bag, and while it "smoked" mimed the utter agony of being burned alive.

And when all was done, there was nothing left to be said as Seamour descended, standing over our desks, barefoot, cold, in a pair of old ripped tan linen pants, with a sullied and nipple-shadowed white t-shirt. Hovering above our seats, solitary as Noah's dove, assessing the damage from the Arc. The whole class stared at Tabitha's head.

I mean Seamour might as well have been bald.

A goose egg.

I slipped out of my seat to sweep those hairs with my hand onto a sheet of notebook paper, feeling like Sieur Louis de Conte. I even put a thick lock discreetly in my shirt pocket.

(And I still have it.)

Without a doubt, that "transgression" moved everyone the most. Like the very slaughtering of maidenhood. Maybe because that part was more real, and we put so much emphasis on hair, how much or how little, on head or body.

So much so like the scholastics argument of how many angels can dance on the head of a pin in the days of Thomas Acquinas. One, or many, and if many, how many? Hair a thing appearing and disappearing by law unknown to us. Angel hair.

Angel hair. That's a strange combination. That's an "actual" substance associated with otherworldly encounters, like UFOs or sightings of the Virgin Mary. The un-reality.

I'll remind that for us hair is plural and singular at the same time. We don't say "I cut my hairs," but hair. Yet, we complain of "splitting hairs," not splitting hair. All and one, as if to emphasize it as "all or nothing."

For added stress.

People lose their crowns from distress. "Cause," unidentifiable. Alopecia. And interestingly asking for Angel hair, as a cut in a salon, is code for:

"I need help."

I started to think in terms of contrast.

All or nothing.

Binary vs nonbinary.

We live in a digital world. Actually, we have always lived in a digital world, one dependent on the hand and fingers, specifically, of man-not-monkey or other animal... Like represented by Adam's touching the mirror tip of God. Or Armstrong, laboring to plant that flag on the Moon... By "man," I'll hurry to elaborate, the definition meant, is mankind.

Humanity.

And our implements.

It's not that we make things. We accumulate.

The inanimate... the *Lifeless*.

Even as we have ventured into the virtual world, invisibly, we have accumulated the binary code of 0's and 1's. Dual. Mentally. Like something must always be in opposition. Interestingly, studies have shown actual anatomical difference of the male and female brain— in humans and other animals. Differing in structure/ function by sex.

The brain itself is bipartite.

It isn't necessarily war.

Yet, I'm seeing the nonbinary as something like a statement against that dichotomy.

"Everything is dying," Seamour would say.

True enough. That is the foundation isn't it. Life and Death. More so than Good or Bad. More than any other contrast. But not everything in the world is killing itself off. Negating. I think that was Sean's point. To accept or enhance, but to well enough leave alone the core. The source.

At lunch, Sean had added:

"Like if you have an accident, dude, look you *need* plastic surgery, amiright? and if you don't, it's like playing with your own shit."

...As opposed to playing with clay, which is, essentially, you know, somebody else's shit.

"Seriously, man, you know everybody jerks off!" jabbed Deontay, with a finger to the chest. Sean made a Sooo-Shocked-Face and Elijah snorted milk out the nose, the three of them pushing and shoving, on their side of the cafeteria table, and we let it go.

I wasn't cross-dressing yet at that point. And growing my hair out, later, was frowned upon mostly by adults, and on run-ins with new kids occasionally. But it was nothing. For me.

Elizabeth and Sarah worried, though, as things progressed. As Moms are apt to do.

I overheard them once. I had been intent on running over to Seamour's one Spring and it was raining. I just missed the opening drizzle and found myself standing at the screen door facing a sheet of torrential downpour. A bridal veil in the change of season. They must have thought I'd made it out just before the deluge.

"Do you think we should say something?"

"Oh, now I don't know. These things are a passing phase, we all have to go through, and test our limitations. I think it's character building. Do you remember the summer you walked on stilts, all the time? You refused to take them off and Mom and Dad were furious. They said you'd break your legs and everything in and out of the house!"

"Yes, but I'm concerned... about others."

"Others?! Others are going to think what they're going to think, aren't they? And I say let them. What counts is the kind of person you are inside, and sometimes that is going to be tested. To be strengthened, I might add."

"I'm not worried about character, Lizzie. I'm worried about physical person."

"Physical person? Well, we can just thank our lucky stars, then, that Jenny isn't into hair dying, body piercings, tattoos, and that god-awful thing young people do nowadays, pushing their earlobes around those big plastic loops. Or unwashed dreadlocks, or not bathing or shaving at all, like some hippies used to do. Jenny doesn't wear makeup or dress like a tramp, if that's what has you all in a bunch."

"I worry it could come to some physical altercation."

"Physical altercations!? You mean a fight. I just don't see Jenny in a fight with anybody, really, I don't."

"That's not what I mean."

"Hmph. Goodness, I think you're underestimating our child altogether. If they ever sensed anything disagreeable, they would walk away. Seamour, too. I'm sure of it. We all lean towards nonviolence here, even Irving. Isn't that right, sweetie?"

I could picture Elizabeth fattening Irving up and Sarah's brow furrowing.

They were right on all accounts.

The rain subsided, and I crossed the lingering drops, the edge of my hem soaked by the time I reached Seamour's house.

I've never been particularly religious. Turned out my Moms were Baptist. They made no effort to convert me to church going, but they talked about God and the Bible more often than not.

With reverence.

My dispersed childhood wasn't suited for instilling consistent or effective religiosity. I'd read the Bible out of curiosity. And it was hard reading. Like poetry. Dad referenced it. So did Holdan. In fact, Holdan had gotten pretty conservative, like reborn even, and sent Tabitha straight through Catholic Sunday school from first grade. Right up until the moment of confirmation— at which point it turned out they weren't ready.

"Well, I *can* do it, but would that be following the commandments?"

Seamour had questions. We both did.

Raised as I was, I have no problem seeing God in three persons, as well as Omnipotent, the Everything and Void, the Animating force of the Greater Nothing.

However it is you want to phrase: The Is. The Am. The I. The ?

.

Seamour for a long while couldn't get passed the
—Why?

Why does God allow suffering? Disease, war, pain? Why does God give and take?

It made me picture this Ogre of a custodian with some clanking hoop of heavy keys to Heaven and Hell, and a trailing pail-and-mop cart of reality and fantasy, odd containers of various harsh cleaning agents, and giant black plastic sacks for garbage.

 A literary device, in or out of Canon.

God, it seems, is also an unreliable narrator. Or we only see and hear what we chance. I can't say, "want to," that would assume more choice than I accept.

Seamour gave me Hawthorne's short story, "The Minister's Black Veil" to read one night. I couldn't help but feel that was something of the way God is viewed— ever behind a dark Veil— like that mysterious Minister, even till death. "There," as made present by Material Emblem of darkness, but never really "known."

Except that nobody was actually asking to *See God*. What they wanted was to *Hear God*.

An Explanation.

It was as if Nathanial was suggesting even in Death, that Black Veil remained segregating: the World, You, God. The human condition, as it were.

I remembered then that that was the name of the invasive plant in our yard: Hawthorne. It was that hedge that needed deheading, lest it proliferate all over in tiny overreaching briars.

Hawthorne was not a transcendentalist. Not like say, Ralph Waldo Emerson, with the notion of looking deep inside for spiritual guidance, because of an inherent goodness to be found in there, for us all. Or by escaping to Walden Pond, like Thoreau. Going off to live in the woods alone seems like a good idea when feeling lost.

Spiritually.

You know, Self-connect.

Soon after I handed Seamour the Vedas. An old tattered copy I had given to Dad originally. Giving a thing to Tabitha always meant it would be slowly, but surely, ingested.

My main question: Why are we concerned with God?

Should it matter?

"I just get the feeling people, as a group, are looking for some kind of loophole."

"Like Holy Wars?"

"A dupe."

None of the things that guide ethical conduct are at all based on faith, it seems. Like does God necessarily need to exist and decree that "it's wrong to Lie," or do I know that by effect?

Do I blame God, or some other boogiemen, for consequences of my own actions, or simply acknowledge that consequences exist? Or maybe that God is Consequence.

Like *with sequence*.

Or at least our Living experience (God as we know) is with sequence. Consciousness. Birth to Death. And the other side is blank. To us.

Sometime later, I was bumbling along the sidewalk thinking on this awareness, making my way from Holdan's and Tabitha's to the library. I mean Seamour's. It was getting dark, but I wanted to trace the etymology of consequence and was wondering if cycle had any tie in, or whether end is a must. Like death.

Consequi? A random wondering.

I was very absorbed between the hemispheres of my brain on this and only caught a flash towards me from the side alley shadows.

"What are you wearing?" a rather touched man, around mid-twenties, in gray tweed cabbie hat was peering into my face way too close all the sudden, like we were at some red-carpet runway gala. And from behind swooped in some pock marked side kick with ruddy hair, to the right. Then a third. Dark tied back hair with mirror bug-eye like sunglasses, surfaced on the left, at my elbow.

Like paparazzi.

"Oh, my, my! The Doll has on Versace, isn't it?" said a high-pitched voice holding out an imaginary microphone, pushing up a pair of oversized tinted glasses.

"Or is it Gucci goo? Babe, where are you going out on the town all alone?" the first one, walking backwards now right in front of me, thumbs inserted into belt buckle loops of conspicuously tight black jeans.

"Ladies and Gents, we have got ourselves here a *gen-u-wine* Barbie. Whwet whooh! Doesn't even talk," said Ruddy, clapping me on the back. I imagined that next would be a slap on the backside. My imagination was quicker than any action.

Pause of breath— I went through fisticuffs, a bloodied lip, torn clothes, the brink of rape. In a matter of imaginary seconds.

Ok, I was naïve. And, Elizabeth and Sarah were right. I'd never fought a physical fight.

I'm going to take this moment to God bless TV. Imitation if not instinct kicked in. I tripped the one at my right, who went flying into the one in front, toppling each other, and simultaneously swung my leather satchel into the face at left. All of this was accompanied by a horrific high pitched shriek and fear driven adrenaline.

But truly, I was saved by the Light.

A floodlight turned on in the building nearest, and the taunters scattered. I pulled my skirt down over the red tights Seamour had been so fond of years ago. Amazing how they always stretched to fit. An elderly couple emerged, cautiously, out from the darkened doorway. Gruffly, I heard:

"Goodness, Sweetheart, are you all right?" and seeing the kind extension of an aged worker's hand, I turned my very late noonday shadow to accept the gentleman's outreach.

I'd gotten fairly tall and thinly muscular.

Eye contact.

Instant retraction.

"What the phf! Ella get back in the house! Ugh, how dare you. Gross. Perverse! All of you. Perverts and degenerates! Get outta here! You hear, man? Git."

I ran. I was sure the next step was getting a dog or a gun. Sooner or later. Like maybe they'd now be prompted to buy one, or the other, if they didn't already have both.

I made it to the Library.

I visualized myself looking something like Mother in Psycho. Hair and dress askew, as stretched thin as Anthony Perkins. It amused me. I couldn't help but grin crookedly, passing the long windows. I scratched the stubble.

The release of tension resulted in a wicked humor, and some introspection. Seamour and I had taken up this whole task, willfully, but not like white man's burden. Not to convert others by preaching or enlisting anyone into a dubious cause.

Self-reflection. That's all.

The Self is all encompassing.

I opened up the gigantic old-school hardcover latest edition of the Complete and Unabridged Dictionary of the English Language.

We wanted only to demonstrate to ourselves that we were not the materia. Others would maybe see that, in our consistency. That the point that made us "us" was outside the grasp of our physicality. Hovering apart. A part. Going to extreme, that without face or appendage, between head and heart and stomach, living and breathing, I could still be pinned as "me."

Even with a sex change. Theoretically.

Sorry Sean.

Consequi it turned out meant "to achieve."

Present active infinitive. I decided it's cyclical after all not quite sequential. We are always in the process of, not finally achieving, till death. Maybe the concentricity is irregular, like maybe the circle is sometimes bigger, sometimes smaller, but a cycle, nevertheless.

I didn't tell Sarah and Elizabeth.

I had forgotten my phone. I made a mental note not to do that again—I didn't have a death wish.

And I certainly didn't want my Moms worrying, and fussing, over my well-being. Physically.

Mentally, I had to get used to living all together again. When Dad was ill over the years I got used to doing a lot of things on my own. Like grocery shopping, or runouts for books or medicine. Suddenly, yard work or food shopping was a social activity. With Sarah and Elizabeth, I mean. They took their time. I realized that I ran errands, and it was basically a hold on my "life." No such thing. My Moms made me rethink the waste.

They talked and I listened.

"I've been noticing more and more glitches in the newsreels. Have you caught that, too? I read those little interferences are indicators that a video is not a live stream but is actually CGI or other hi res animation, and it made me own up to just how these broadcasts can be doctored, more easily than live video."

"You mean at a point later."

"Yes, well sooner or later, in history, like for what's called revisionism, or power mongering agenda. You don't know, dearie, but Sarah is a journalist." The bright store lights glimmered off the lanyard cheerily.

"Retired," said affably, but with a contained smile.

"Mhm, once a journalist, always a journalist at heart, is what I'd say. There's a whole file no one is allowed to touch. You don't even know where it is. Yet," Elizabeth baited. And I was curious.

"Investigative?"

"Journalism," Sarah said curtly. I got it. Like what true journalism isn't, right? Investigative.

On the ride back, Sarah and Elizabeth chatted quietly amongst themselves in front till we were almost home.

My mind wandered. I could see Seamour walking down a side street, back towards me. It occurred to me that whatever Tabitha put on, it was only the clothes that could be said to be androgynous. I guess it was the gait that made me think that.

The roll of the hips.

13. morning sickness

I'm sure I talk too much.

Seamour's only vice is chocolate.

Tabitha never really struggled with weight, not more than our average youth going through growth spurts, filling and evening out. So, when I point it out, it's not what you'd think. And it's not the sugar. Diabetes or ADHD. Nor am I going on again about poor teeth. Everybody ought to have their teeth pulled and those porcelain implants screwed in—save everybody the trouble. The pain. Really, imagine the expense and agony saved if we all got it done. Level the playing field as well, for the dazzling Madamn America smile. Human species, judging by rotting teeth and failing eyesight isn't exactly getting any stronger or keener.

Powdering our noses makes no difference.

I've digressed.

It's just that cacao is full of antioxidants as it is in heavy metal. Metals like cadmium and lead. You don't let your kids drink from the tap if the levels tip 15 ppb. And yet we pay three to eight bucks for a deluxe bar.

With heavy metals.

I told Tabitha, who then pointed out to me that it's common knowledge that a lot of magnesium is needed for the menstrual cycle (exkuse me) and anytime really to maintain life balance. That a person can go for several days without water but will actually perish in hours without magnesium.

No shortage, apparently, standing here as we were, living and eating, and I continued to argue cautiously for brain over ova.

"There are many ways to take a bullet," Seamour said.

So, yeah there are worse ways to go. But I will add for all the benefits... the serotonin, OxyContin, aphrodisiac effect... chocolate has the same compound as marijuana.

And then, I wonder, hmm, they don't call that shit "dope" for nothing...

"Pick a different snack."

"I'm going to do what I'm going to do," they said.

Seamour had some absurd reasoning about nothing "killing appetite" like dark chocolate. Eating being a time-consuming nuisance. Like sitting on the toilet.

The gross charcoal 100% baking cacao would do as well, if not better, than gold foiled candy.

I'm inclined to think taste had nothing to do with the consumption. Like a smoker starts with menthol as an aesthetic masking and then has no quals switching to undressed regular.

Being hooked.

So, when she, I mean, they started holding their stomach and acting like they were going to hurl, rushing to the bathroom, I figured the gross reality of this irrational indulgence finally introduced itself, and the gag reflex would properly fix the chocoholic.

Of course it wasn't "the only thing" they ate.

It sticks out the most though.

Seamour had started complaining also about not being able to eat anything sweet.

If I'd been from a large family it might have tipped me off with alarms. My father was really the only relative I'd known, closely, and Dad had died of late diagnosed cirrhosis. Food became a major consideration. Actually, more of a preoccupation in our lives.

There was the notion of "how to eat right," while holding tender the little pleasant socially known evils. Which boiled down, in the process of elimination (as what one cannot absolutely go without), at least from what I could tell, to arthritic latte and cancerous cigarettes.

And between these two, in the final months of dying food and cigarettes trailed.

Coffee won. Black.

As the last to be had before death.

So, if you're curious, I'll try to keep it brief, but thorough.

The regiment consisted of not only what you eat but in what combination, as well as timing of day, and while this might seem like a chore to remember, think of it as orthodoxy and it soon becomes matter of course in meal planning.

The axiom underlying is that We eat to Live, Not live to Eat... while remembering that Enjoyment is important to Psychological Nutrition:

*Thou Shalt Keep Fruits and Starchy Vegetables Separate.

*Thou Shalt Keep Starches and Proteins Separate.

*Take Sugar with sugar, Early in the day, and/or Never after Fat, Starch or Protein meal.

*Take Starch with Vegetables. Protein with Non-Starchy Vegetables. Fats with either.

*Oh, and Keep it simple.

*As in Four or Less ingredients at a meal.

*No expressed Fats, in mass amount as unnatural as processed sugar.

*And keep it Raw.

*Or lightly steamed if absolutely necessary.

*Two or three meals a day. 4-6 hours betwixt meals.

Amen.

Seamour and I had this acquired food faith oddly in common for the most part. Except that I had been indoctrinated, and they had been seeking.

We paid attention to nutrition. Tabitha didn't eat meat since fourth grade. Well before then, but later, on grabbing some charitable chicken dinner at a friend's house, not to be rude, was woefully reminded, i.e. gastronomically the very next day, that on eschewing meat, the body loses the ability to digest it.

In any case, each of us developed some odd very particular dietary habits. I worried, but I also didn't want to make an even bigger deal of these things.

"You're drinking a lot of water." I noticed.

Seamour had started walking around with this giant ass more than gallon size container. Jocks haul these around for weightlifting as much as for hydration.

Now I've heard that water is good for you, and we often don't "drink enough," but conversely, guzzling water washes out vital nutrients and messes with the pH of the body.

"I got a UTI," Seamour whispered.

I knew what that meant. Clint had announced it to everyone well back in History class in seventh grade, saying, "Hahaha!" in that booming thespian voice, "Now I know what you all girls go through!!"

Massive eye rolls from half the class and laughter, till Kelly jumped up and said: "Wait— are you bleeding even when you're not peeing?!"

That is The difference, right?

"No... I see pink in the bowl when I piss."

Not even red.

Anyway, it should have been another flag.

Athletes get urinary tract infections. It's a sign of dehydration, true enough, but there are other major physical stressors on the body's water supply. Like during illness.

Seamour wasn't exactly the physically active type. As in doing sports.

We walked.

Ok we also biked, but we hadn't in a while.

Come to think of it, Seamour was packing on a few pounds. They were always hungry all the sudden and cranky about it.

It's an irony worth noting that the job I got when my Dad was ill, and I was avoiding Seamour, was at

Flours Bakery. Shifts were favorable, before and after school. And weekends. Total twenty-five hours a week, at minimum wage, which in middle school, was plenty. As a minor, Dad had to sign off on my worker's permit, and I'd had to take a physical. This consisted of me doing a couple jumping jacks and touching my toes.

"Good to go."

...My general practitioner was a Filipino with a thick accent and maybe this exaggerated the perception of quick once over. I had the odd impression if there were factually something wrong with me nobody in the office would recognize it or figure out what it was. Maybe because as a child I suffered eczema and the same doctor said:

"No known cause."

For me or anybody, I'd asked.

"No known cause."

And I got on my way out a small packet of hand lotion. From this age, it's kinda funny. Back then it irritated. I didn't get the joke yet.

Eczema's one of those mystery afflictions, sort of like migraines. Onset brought about by different triggers for different people. I've read since that both have something to do with congestion in the system. Digestive or lymphatic.

A kind of backup.

Worst kind is "creative constipation," as Seamour says. Or maybe, emotional.

The Bakery was industrial. If you're imagining I did some kind of baking or cooking—the simplest mix and stir—no. That was all mechanized. Vats received Ready-Mix-Packs poured in through a chute from a mini-silo. That was filled up by white impersonal culinary dump trucks. The vat rotated like a cement mixer, while a small funnel at the bottom released every last drop... drop by drop onto an industrial steel tray. The trays then slid, one at a time, into the bottom of the commercial oven through a narrow slot at the bottom, like an air vent. Each layer added beneath the other on tiers something like in a hamster wheel, rotating the trays in the gas heated chamber.

What then was my function?

Apparently, some shortage in automatization. Either lack of money or parts. I was packing by hand. The resulting small spongy poofs, injected with vanilla or chocolate shortening, had to be slipped into plastic wrappers. The baggies had an adhesive strip. So, from the conveyor belt, I'd grab a poof, slide it into the sleeve, remove the paper tab, and fold the sticky flap ever so gently, and quickly set it into a box that was rolling away from me into a hole in the wall where presumably on the other side it was getting sealed and shipped out. Probably to gas stations.

Or grocery marts.

There was nobody to ask.

There were ten of us and each of us knowing nothing. It was not difficult to tell. We all seemed to fit into some stereotype of reliable ignorance. I as child-worker... Antonio, Jesus, Henrietta, and Carmen as non-English speaking immigrants. Edgar and Susanne were cognitively impaired. Stephen, Daria and Jayce were all addicts, spaced by drugs and/ or alcohol.

I showed up like clockwork and I could easily gage our attendance and alertness on the job. Poor, with tardiness, absenteeism and cutting out early.

The main hours of operation were 8am to 5pm. This extra that was being squeezed out was bonus time, after hours, or so it seemed.

I got the job site and persons unseen, and kept it till CPS yanked me. I had answered an IMMEDIATE HIRE post in the newspaper. I pictured a short, fat middle-aged New Yorker of indeterminate descent. Thinning hair swept to the right over a balding scalp. Thick fingers, smoking. In filthy white apron.

Probably not. More likely, sports coat.

"Yeah, I got a couple openings. Can you do an hour or two starting at 5:30? A.M."

"Yes. Absolutely. I can do 5:30 to 7a.m., every day. Plus evenings," I heard some scribbling on scratch paper.

"Great. Great, weekdays. And weekends? I need about ten hours on weekends."

"Sure."

"—you sure? You start tomorrow."

14. Fear

I was the one to tell Holdan.

I didn't even feel like a traitor by then. I needn't.

Seamour was acquiescent.

"I can go. You can go. Or we can both go," I said, already decided in action.

We went.

"Well," said Holdan, "well." And the answers to all the obvious questions seemed equally obvious there under the green lamp shade of the center table that made the room look like more of a study than kitchen.

Except for one unasked question.

"They're not ok," I answered.

"I'll take you."

We drove, all three of us, soundlessly.

I texted my Moms: *Going with Seamour to the clinic.*

Tabitha hadn't actually met my Moms till after the adoption was official. After I'd run off, I was placed back in that first host home. They worked out transportation, and I saw Seamour at school again weekdays.

What to call them?

"It all depends on the relationship you form," they said. As might be obvious, to given names neither of us was strongly committed. I've forgotten to say, that of course, Seamour called Holdan, "Holdan," not Dad or anything else like that. And Mom, for Tabitha, was a picture in a frame, lovingly inscribed Beatrice, unknown since birth. And Holdan had never remarried.

I felt no fear in the prospect of adoption. I mean, in abstraction yes, but not when I met my Moms. We were people. Just people. Sure, at different points of Life. Maybe it will be cynically criticized that I had a vested interest. To get out, go back home, reclaim something of ownership.

Autonomy.

Home was not a motivator, but it was a bonus.

I liked them quickly. For their goodness. What solidified for me a place in my heart for my Moms was the surprise that waited for me the day they took me out of the county assigned host home. To their house, three minutes' drive from Brook Ave.

It was Irving.

They had adopted my dog first.

"We knew nothing about you, then, isn't that something?" Elizabeth beamed over steaming hot Jasmine infused white tea poured out in little pale pink floral oriental porcelain teacups with no ears.

Sarah smiled: "Irving ran away."

"We drove around in the Acura, and I spotted that chunky tan body nuzzled against that great big yellow entrance door of yours. No head, kind of ostrich style, it was the most heart wrenching thing. Perked ears up right away and came back to us when we called out, though."

Taking a sip, Sarah smiled bigger, with a shake of the head, "That's when we started to put things together."

"Maybe, just maybe, this was the dog that poor child had lost, and we looked back in our paperwork from the pound. You know, to check the 'former owner' section. They had given reason for impoundment as '…abandoned by owner…' Scandalous! The owner's last name was same we realized as yours, you know, the name of that poor child that had been put into a group home after being found living all alone."

Sarah smiled with me, fit to break: "Sorry we didn't tell you."

I wasn't. Sorry, I mean.

It would have changed the order of things. Would have called into question rationale, motivation. Premeditation, maybe. I would have doubted the purity of my own emotions.

"Calculation," Seamour said.

Most dogs wag their tails, Pitbulls wiggle their whole backside. Irving greeted me like Lazurus. Yelping, licking, butt wiggling. The Moms were very proud. They'd done well.

Next to Tabitha, Irving was blood.

But I'm getting ahead of myself.

I filled Seamour in on all the bullshit leading up to everything till now. Naturally, we were for a fraction of an hour put out.

"I understand why you didn't tell me," Tabitha said softly running a hand across the hoodie in self-soothing, taking two breaths in, one long sigh out.

They had taught me that it's not about the in, as much as it is about the breath out. I know dammit, if I had memorized their number, I could've called from the first host home. Seamour didn't mention it, tactfully. In consideration for our backlog. And the idea of letting go... of bullshit I suppose.

"Do you know when you exhale you're removing waste from spent carbohydrates?"

I guess I'd never really thought about where the carbon comes from, when we're inhaling oxygen and exhaling carbon dioxide. They also mentioned too much breathing in upsets the oxygen balance in the bloodstream, and brain, consequently.

Timing is the thing.

Too much, hyperventilation.

Too little, suffocation.

I've been near fainting. And it's terrifying. I imagine it's something like near death. I lost a lot of pounds in those ten months of wait. Naturally, it had already begun, prior. Like I said, when my Dad was ill I wasn't thinking of taking care of me. It continued, like a breath withheld, once I was caught in the system. Not knowing what would happen.

I was standing in the kitchen, peeling an apple of all things, and I cut my thumb. Deep. No one else was in at the time. None of us kids. No hosts.

I said, "Oh my god, oh my god," like a full-on convert, and covered one thumb with the other. Nothing was coming out. The blaspheming was prophylactic. I made it to the bathroom medicine cabinet. You know the mirror behind the sink. I saw my pale face, and thought spontaneously, *Jesus Christ.* When I say deep, the cut was diagonal to my thumb, and ran straight through the fingernail, almost out the other side.

The temporary foster family had those Japanese steel knives. Overkill, I'd say, but I couldn't find the peeler. And sure, it struck me really odd that this kind of "housing situation" would even open up that kind of risk for "mistake."

I'd actually finished removing all of the skin. I had placed the naked fruit on the counter and was about to split it in half. Maybe I did a little hiya karate chop. Silently. And slipped, with a swift sharp precise notch. On the bias, across the nail. I stared in horror. It was the absence of immediate blood that shocked. But I counted my blessings, and petitioned the lord, as I said rightly or wrongly.

When I got to the bathroom, my face was greyed. I used my nose and chin to pry open the cabinet. Now, I had a problem. How to grab the Band-Aid? Never mind get it open. Unwrap it, or stick it on.

I used my mouth, grotesquely maneuvering lip and jaw in the cabinet, like a cow, I grabbed the box and tucked it under my elbow, shuffled it a little lower till I could rest it on the edge of the pedestal sink. The box, as luck would have it, was sloppily ripped open. I slipped my pinky and ring finger in as pincers. Still squeezing my thumb between my opposite thumb and index.

Painstakingly, I managed to extract like four or five Band-Aids. Exact precision or neatness of debris isn't on anybody's mind in these situations. Is it? I fluttered the strips one by one into the sink, till at last only one remained. Barely in my grasp. I used my teeth to rip it open. And my teeth again to pull the tab. With maniacal precision, I adhered that one tab. Quickly let go and yanked the other tab down.

Success.

I put everything away discreetly. You see, I didn't lose my head, yet. Though in that final moment, I did see blood start to run. My insides were churning, but I was still ok. In mind and body. All the way until late that evening when the host home dad decided "let's have a looksee," and determined to remove and change the bloody band-aid.

The whole top of the thumb was swollen black, blue, purple. And it was then I felt the whole world receding. My hearing went first. Or so it seemed. It was probably my breath that actually went first. The lack of oxygen, involuntary, or cut blood flow. Voices receded far, far off, tapering away. Light dimmed. A colorless gray rose, blackening swiftly. Awareness rising, that I'd probably had "really" needed stitches.

"Water," I heard an internal rasp say: "water!"

A hand handed me a transparent leaden glass and I sipped a heavy liquid. Everything stopped fading. And I felt tremendous relief. A mental crawl back towards life. Tonal differentiation returned from the dim graveyard of sight and sound.

I refused the suggestion of going to a doctor.

At this point, I insisted, the cut would heal just as well on its own... I was extra careful, and it did. Without a scar.

Except as memory.

It's the gray that stuck with me. There's a whole phenomenon. The Gray Man. Tabitha and I hadn't heard of this. I'm sure it would have intrigued Seamour to no end. The whole RAS mechanism. Reticular Activating System. I know, I know, right sounds shitty. But gimme a second. Reticular not recticular. It has to do with the eyes, meaning the brain. It flipped a switch for me later.

Tabitha and I focused on the Conspicuous.

Our childishness was showing. If we could do it all over again, I know Seamour would have pressed instead for Inconspicuousness. This is where the Gray Man comes in.

Or maybe even the Gray Matter.

You see how evolutionary. Socially. We have come from, theoretically, gender and racial segregation to broader and broader inclusion of our many parts. Parsing a whole Rainbow of People, men and women and children.

Yet the mind craves something else.

"Don't you ever wish to be invisible?"

Yes. Seamour was right there. We just never took that path, consciously. The RAS is the part of the brain near the brain stem, just before the spinal cord. Essentially a multiwire pack of neurons, about the circumference of your pinky. All the sensory data (taste, touch, smell, hearing and sight) pass through. Filtered. The RAS doesn't trip any alarm, to trigger a higher-level brain function (meaning Awareness), unless a thing is "off." Odd. The weird subject or object doesn't fit into criteria that allows for quick ID. Known danger. Unknown danger. Known comfort.

A thing desired.

A loss.

The Gray, as I'll shorten it, is what escapes notice. It doesn't trip the security wire. It causes no fear or anxiety or discomfort. As such, is so neutral as to be there. And not. Like heartbeat. Or breath.

But it can also be that person. That you'll have to dig for into subconscious. The one that was at the park. There. In something like a gray sweater, or sweats, or pants, walking. Andante is the musical term, moving along, neither fast nor slow. Doing nothing out of the ordinary. Probably, killing time with their nose in a cell.

The setup is likely making you think— Terrorist! because of our hyper focus nowadays, social politically. But in the moment, not at all. The mind is registering, and dismissing, registering and dismissing. The insignificant encounter logged as one word. On the tip of the tongue, really. And there's an alluring beauty in that very anonymity...

"Well? what then was it?! You must've seen something—" surely, pen hovering over pad. Waiting. Expectantly.

...*What was it? I don't know,* you say, panicked in retrospect. Silently. Furtively searching the scene. All the shadowy corners. Replaying moment by moment. Tracing steps. Putting yourself there. Observer. Observed. A wall of gray. I don't know...

It was...

It was...

"Just a person."

That's what we want to say.

And I know I still need to tell you about Evangeline.

I don't understand why but it's different when you know it's a "girl." No, that's not it. When it's brought vividly to attention and then neutered. Extinguished visually.

This is a tight rope to tread.

Of course, I knew what Seamour was, is or isn't, or wasn't. I mean, Tabitha. Or myself for that matter.

Bear with me.

I don't know if I can accurately describe the twist in my mind. Because, I transposed what I know. I mean, for a split second, it could've been Tabitha. Not factually. Theoretically. When I saw Evangline, in the emergency room, it made me question everything. How far is too far? And had we, I do mean Seamour and I, somehow been culpable.

Indirectly.

Yes, this was "just a person" lying in the gurney. It was an ICD-10. E956. I didn't immediately know what that was at the time. As a number.

I knew what it was. As a person.

15. Announcement

You know jenny is also a female donkey.

An ass.

Seamour pointed that out to me once everything blew over and the facts were on the table and the only thing left was to deal with the new order of things, upcoming.

I got the letter in the mail mid-summer. I'd dragged my feet about sending applications. But I sent out two. And I received a yes back from a school about an hour away, thinking I'd fit together a couple related majors under the Individualized Studies option. Keep doors open. All seemed doable.

"Have you visited?" Seamour asked quietly, after a long silence.

"No."

"What do your Moms think?"

"They want me to choose by myself."

With some additional nudging, from Sarah and Elizabeth, I went. And, as much as I would have poo-poohed anyone else for judging a place on looks, I suddenly was all concerned about feeling and appearances.

Seamour said: "If it doesn't feel right, it isn't."

Know it all.

Separate schools weighed on us gravely. It was expected. All of us were expected to graduate. We were expected to do college. We were expected to graduate and enter gainful employ. The separation was built in. We did what we could to dismiss it. We didn't talk about it. Actually, we talked less and less, even as we met up during usual stops.

We dug our heels in about certain things.

We now called Holdan "they," as well. Not sure why that was the hardest for me. Holdan's such an institution that my mind foolishly "holds" onto as a relic of an order, one that was to be sure was already then in the process of rearranging.

Nevertheless.

They stopped me from the office den at the bottom of the stairs one day: "Jenny, do you have a sec..?" Removing spectacles and wiping the lenses on a corner of a beige cotton cardigan, they looked tired.

Haggard, is the word.

Yes, sir, I wanted to say but only waited in ascent.

"Jenny, well now, you've received a letter...? Congratulations!" Cough, cough and then, a muddled, "has, er, have you... has... er, do you know if," ...cough, cough, cough... "Received any letter?"

Seamour's communication had deteriorated all around. And I was aware of it painfully in this asthmatic reaction on behalf of Seamour's future.

My Dad had died. Tabitha and Holdan's talk was dying over these years.

"I don't know," I said.

If anything, the letter was F.

And if Seamour was ill, I did not want to betray confidence. As a friend, I would not have done that to me. I'd wait. I'd wait. I think. Just like I'd respected my Dad's preferences.

Some shred of evidence was needed to draw any conclusions, and I had nothing, only that Seamour had changed. Incrementally. We could all see that. Retreating from the world. Even, I had changed, and what crime was there in that? We were growing. Up, I suppose. Our view on being minor was skewed by impudence. Legal age has never been a meter of responsibility or under-standing. We were Old(er).

I'm sure I had the impression (wrong) that I'd already experienced a lot. That my struggles counted for something. Like a credit. I don't know. Seamour had been walking along side but on separate tracks. It wasn't that we were growing apart. We were slower in processing things. In judging. We kept quieter.

I had a fierce sense of responsibility, though.

It bordered on possessiveness, but without envy. Seamour, or Tabitha rather, belongs to me. I can't put parameters on it. Whatever the capacity. And if Tabitha wanted space, space was what I was going to give. With all sincerity. I wanted for us to work out whatever's ahead of us. Of us. Even if it meant we're walking along different paths. For whatever unspecified time frame. I mean, hand-holding isn't a physical thing necessarily. Though I've nothing against.

I was failing in understanding.

And my resolve was cracking. I had no idea if they had even applied anywhere, never mind got an acceptance, or rejection. Tabitha never really had dead set plans. Since childhood, I mean. But this silence was getting invasive. We wanted to know.

.

It's weird. You can be walking with someone and not know the points that are defining their life. Or life choices. The things you think are important are ones you have in your own headlights. You're sitting and watching the same movie, against a backdrop of different filters. It's like if someone is terminally ill, every little moment is colored with that information. Or if they are going away, starting over. And haven't made an announcement yet... Or if they've committed a crime.

A secret. They know and you don't.

Silence is tainted.

I imagined a direct approach. Fine, I'd ask.

I'd just ask Tabitha the next time we were walking to school: *is there something troubling you?* We walk every day. The guilt of open opportunities weighed on me. Then, I would counter queasily— if they are ready to share they will. They always do.

I'll ask during lunch: *is there something I can help you with?* We meet up for lunch every day. Except the odd couple of times either of us had an errand to run, but likely we went together, anyway, so no real excuse there... for either of us.

Is there something wrong?

Seamour would have to explain. This time I was going to breach this goddam silence. It happened without me, as if, on the way home on a Friday.

"Tabitha! Tabitha!!" I said quickly clamping both shoulders into my palms and resisting the urge to shake. Idiot, my cheeks flushing crimson at the "mistake."

Unwitnessed as it was.

My heart raced and a cold sweat lined my armpits. I was horrified at the totality of it. When you don't know what's going on, there's that feeling of spiraling away. I suspected illness, drugs, or both.

Seamour had fainted, and I panicked.

The body fell with a dull thud on the soft grassy slope in the yard. We'd been walking and talking, and I'd finally brought up "Holdan's concern" about college. Certainly, I didn't want to agitate directly and had sandwiched it in an invite to visit the Registrar's office of the school that I determined to go to, wanting to avoid the one that creeped me out with the big glass buildings covered with opaque, black, hand painted open-winged raven silhouettes, meant to scarecrow real birds away.

When I first saw it, the whole building shatter...

And then the dead birds splattered, below, like the ones that periodically flew, to their death, into our kitchen sliding door. Wrens.

An ambiguous they. Far gone.

Seamour came-to unaware of my gaffe.

"We're pregnant," they whispered.

16. what to tell Who

Finding a thing is an interesting proposition.

An object once lost quickly forfeits owner ship. We say: "finders keepers," and weigh whether the extra burden, and clutter, is worth it. More often than not, the found thing is consumed, or summarily, let go.

Is it Useful? That is the criteria. Isn't it?

I remember a sign posted in a restroom, it read THINK before you speak. An acronym.

It continued:

...is it T- True?

...is it H-Helpful

...is it I-Inspiring

...is it N-Necessary

... is it K-Kind?

We find all sorts of things coming out from us and coming at us. Without giving it much thought.

I once found a letter D pendant, not even gold or plated. Some fancy old dame rubbish. D. Ornate oldness emanated from it and that had me putting it from pocket to pocket. I dunno. I speculate that it might be also because one of Seamour's grand mothers' name is Dorthy or Dorthea... that vague reference of familiarity clung to me, beyond the letter, or thing itself. I thought about illness and passing away.

I would not own the letter. D.

It's an odd thing how we take possession of our first initial as soon as we learn the alphabet. A is for apple, and that, that, is *My Letter*. Whatever it says on the birth certificate.

That.

There was a time I would have incorporated the trinket into some sculpture. But in the end, I tossed it out. Unceremoniously, directly into the trashcan.

They find babies in dumpsters.

The frame of mind that goes with that dump is hard to even begin to examine. The dumper sees *things. Not persons*— Not self, not an Other. Ejecting foreign matter out of the body. Whatever part of self, or whoever (related to self), that offended. Tossed out because of perceived error. And more so, fear. It's odd, medically, I've learned since that in labor the moment where the baby comes out is formally called Expulsion, and all the umbilical cord that trails behind, after, is called "Birth of the Placenta."

Weird, right. Words have melody, harmonics. Ideas attracted each other. Like people. Or so I always thought.

I've fought off anorexia and bulimia. Bringing them to my own consciousness. That needs to happen before "denial." And I know that these kinds of disorders can happen to any body. Same as when deep depression hits. As a battle between the physical and mental. It's a pretty dangerous thing to say, indignantly: No, how could Somebody?! ....Because that somebody could even be you. It happens insidiously.

As a gradual not sudden decline.

We don't recognize the little steps preceding in the onset of our psychological autoimmune-like ailments that gnaw away at body from the inside.

The distortion in cause and effect. We don't see. We maintain. That it's "ok."

Image, I mean. And imagination.

Once I knew of the pressure Seamour was holding in, the heft of what and how and when, I worried about either of us getting sick. In all ways. The mind is monstrous in the things it dredges up. People fall into Hate. Against themselves, more than anyone.

More than we ever fall in Love.

In our repeated fantasies we are plastic surgeons, examining this or that, practicing our self-hatred. Designing what should go, what should stay, and what needs "fixing." And it's not all about looks. Deeper down, it's that pivotal question, *does it get me what I want:*

"Is it Useful?"

Not helpful, inspiring, necessary, or kind.

Seamour says folks are still fascinated with the Bobbit case, because so many harbor a socially rooted fear, or hatred even, of the male member, for its function, "for the way it burdens."

With Life. Life consequences. Yeah, I get that.

Barbie likewise—the crotchless, permanently bra-and-girdle molded figure—is near and dear to hearts as the object of unattainability:

Sterile plastic.

What Seamour expressed as:

"...The desired inconsequence of being."

As we grew, I wanted to play with Tabitha's dolls. I remember that hot summer, at Holdan's, out by their old underground pool near the semi-circular driveway. Swimming in XXL t-shirts and sweating to death. Each of us absconding the water, for shame of showing our awkward prepubescent bodies. We took the Barbies skinny dipping. They were props in an art video we'd conjured up.

"Why'd you chop off all their hair?" I asked.

"Seems they should be bald," pointing to the genitals and up, "I mean, their labia and nipples have been left out why leave hair?" Seamour said.

We took sandpaper and acetone and wiped off their faces as well.

You know. Carry through on the social statement.

I don't know what happened to the vid. The file's probably still on the disk, in the camera. A Nikon.

We called the skit: "Starting from Scratch." We had some audio, but it turned out the mic on the device was broken or something. Maybe water got on it. Maybe I just didn't hit the right setting.

We stopped using the camera after that.

No, it never occurred to us to tape ourselves. That would breach the confidence we kept amongst us. We don't do that. Body image. Branding.

Control.

Not that Tabitha didn't look good. Always. In all ways. Everything that needed to be in place was.

Kept under cover.

Seamour had this long-standing asceticism. The temple is to be honored by minimalism and self-restraint. Discipline. And the fact that the temple body under development was svelte, blessed with aristocratic bone structure, and graced with perky breasts and a round ass was tacitly accepted and unmentioned.

Robing of clothing is curtain to imagination.

I say this cautiously.

Fact was I had seen Tabitha undressing, when we were Freshmen. One of those stupid incidents where curiosity takes over propriety. I knew I shouldn't. I looked. I saw. I filed it into the mental drawer under, "Why?".

I mean, if I had a body like that would I cover it up...

I guess the idea is acceptance. You have what you have, and leave it at that. Ideally. That's what makes the rejection, conscious or not, so difficult. Because, there was without spin, a rejection. Or if not full rejection, a kind of denial. We knew it when the question presented itself in the form of Phae years ago.

In Tabitha's mind, I think it was formed, early on as a question of degree... the Disproportion strongly insinuated. Which half, in broadest brushstroke, of humanity is carrying a burden too big to bear? Where exactly do we need, as if, reinforcement? Or retreat. You know, strategically. Where to take a stand.

Like in battle.

Or a game even. Though I can't think of one that aptly relates to our current oxymoronic "social-isolation." Sure, roleplaying pops to mind. Not the creative make-believe from childhood.

The scripted kind. You assume a character, from a deck of cards, and have certain rules to play by.

Interesting, how important scripting is along the spectrum of our thoughts.

Seamour said low: "I think I understand the idea of action in inaction." Speaking of Arjuna in battle. That choosing not-to is as impactful as choosing-to and the consideration, in "right" human action, is the smallest print: the Impact. Like the side effects on medicine at the very bottom of the label in 2pt font. This was in hospital, when we were talking about acceptance and tolerance.

It occurred to me, at one point, that Joan of Arc might've been something of a straw figure. Maybe. The kind of scarecrow waved over the heads of those who were wavering, needing a kick in the ego to take themselves to task. Look you, pansies! Here is a girl child heading out to war... a girl child! For pity's sake.

But if Seamour and I could have actually switched places, in fact, not fictionally, might it have been easier...? I don't know. We'd have swapped, at least for a moment. I'd have carried that weight for them. The uncertainty. The heavy responsibility of life. No. Of lives.

Life, capital.

Obviously, we couldn't. Can't.

We're given certain things to bear.

The challenge is in our alignment of will with the Greater Will. It wasn't like exchanging our wardrobes. Token ritual, spiritual, an entirely symbolic gesture. It's something like letting go, but holding on, at the same time... Yeah, I did think about it: What if Tabitha had suggested going all the way? Like under the knife.

However, you want to interpret that. In my mind, I've already weighed all the possibilities. Self-mutilation, abortion, suicide...

Disassembling. See how the term is glued? Facts remain facts, regardless of distance.

Even after death.

Clothes do not make the head honcho. And by the same misleading coin, "the crowd treats you how it sees you." Age-old adages, that on our social skin are blinders and Band-Aids. Ripping them off hurts. At some point we all stand in front of the mirror naked.

We felt something. At the time we couldn't name it. A discomfort. But it wasn't actual pain. I could see it also in the faces of others around our age. It took me a while to figure it out.

Name it I mean.

The Potential.

Ours... and the not living up to it. Its presence and its absence. Because I would say potential, in the human mind, is more expansive than any galaxy. The greater the ability to appreciate its existence, the bigger its perceived lack.

An intellectual black hole.

All of us dancing on the frayed outskirts of our "Potential."

When I found out about our pregnancy I didn't see Seamour the same way. I saw, oddly enough, a submarine. A sort of enemy fire rising amidst our water, withholding final blow. It was my heart, remembering sharply that way back Tabitha had been anti. Both.

Birthing. And killing.

I wasn't angry.

I was surprised. Scared. I felt Vacuum.

Sounds idiotic now but it was then that I actually looked up "nonbinary."

17. should we keep It

Yeah, it dawned on me had our timing been otherwise, I'd be writing this from Juvey. It's called Statutory, and as such is condemnation with no fact finding needed. By Law.

I don't even want to enter the word. The crime.

It doesn't fit here.

I'm younger than Seamour. Just a few months. I was seventeen. That was the saving grace within the double standard that would have been for us the "coup de grace."

It was Seamour who was eighteen.

The legal workers went into one of those long closed door meetings. Where you wait to be called in… The doors opened and the attendees were seen, sitting stiff, wan powdered big wigs. The public defender, the social workers, and the judge, all in civilian dress suits, actually.

Costumes, either way.

The public defender had put in an official "stay," due to "extenuating circumstances."

Seamour's assigned legal counselor was a stylish black diva. One of those that people refer to in private circles as up-and-coming. With high heels the counsel towered over Seamour and, putting arms akimbo, gave what looked like an animated low toned diatribe.

I'm not sure what words actually transpired, but I imagined it something like this when those fierce red acrylics wrapped themselves sternly around Tabitha's fallen cheeks and jaw:

"Sweetheart, just wha do yah think yur doin' with yah life? We need to puhl ourself together, ya hear? Just lookatchu chile!"

The voice in rich Southern drawl.

I saw Letoya Cruz cinch up a piece of my old Christmas flannel shirt Seamour had—worn to death—pinched it like it was something foul. It was as tattered as a toddler's security blanket. A tactile contrast to the finely tailored royal blue silk rayon professional-blend that gave a menacing sheen in the office overhead lighting.

I loved Seamour in that plaid multicolor shirt, it was more than clothing. It was second skin.

I knew "chile" by lip movement. I'd heard it fall in castigation on a previous occasion, when Letoya lolled down the corridor hip to hip with a caseworker:

"Lawd wha is with dat beautiful chile?"

Leytoya had those immaculate narrow tight braids elaborately wrapped atop the head like a priestess. Again, I had the impression of being put together. Suddenly, I wanted to see Tabitha put together. Variants ran through my mind. None fit. No, I wanted Seamour just like that, in whatever— but with a genuine smile back.

I didn't want either of us on any sex offenders list.

Leytoya took me aside, with my legal counsel in tow. A bland sniffle of a person, short and scrawny in loose three-piece suit, named Peabody, who I could tell didn't much like to stick a nose out for anybody.

"I don't know whatch ya'all got goin' one here, but I'd like to believe yah two actually love each otha, alright?" Long pause, piercing me in the eye. "Good. So, Baby, I'm gonna go ahead and push for a Romeo and Juliet exception in da brief, 'kay?" Pause. "Do ya understand, hon?"

"Yes Ma'am."

Peabody, nodded along. We signed.

The charge would be graded as misdemeanor. The offense, for Seamour, unless dismissed by the court, could never be expunged. That is the law here.

A tentative hearing date was set.

I realized then that I'm very against secrets. And yet, all my life, I've been their keeper. Family secrets. The confidence of friends. The lock upon my own self. Private. Even Seamour, as you see, knew only so much. As did I, about them.

Sometimes success is believed to be in the hiding of something or other, really well. Storing. Cache. Withholdings. Companies make income that way, don't they?

Maybe it has something to do with stock. Or bonds. This all comes to mind as I'm scrolling through the internet. So much is in there, and I'm being bombarded with advertisements.

Even for a newly released song. The lyrics are catchy and on loop: "Wet 'n juicy, come 'n getch 'ur pussy..." This is followed kitty-corner with infomercial for a new erectile dysfunction med. Huh. Right. Yeah, I've been around long enough now to comprehend the irony.

Explicit, or maybe we should say vulgar, allusion would have been somewhere out there. Pushed to the margins. While publicly, much time's spent culturally beating down the male sex, hatching up the female sex. And then surprise, surprise. There's nobody left, really.

To come or get it, I mean.

Strokers and vibrators. Pills. Lubricators. In mass production. While individuals shift in the discomfort of skin, looking desperately for an out, or a crossing over, it seems.

I sat near a transgender in an office not long ago.

It was just when I went off to College as a part-time student. I was sitting at the Registrar's office about to finalize some paperwork for the next semester's schedule. I had decided to refocus. On Life. Sarah and Elizabeth were pleased I'd got pulled together and prioritized. I was checking the times, to make sure there were no conflicts.

There are always conflicts. I mean you want more than you can take, inevitably. Then, even in the "limit," you take more than you can manage, because there is other life stuff. And then you're glad, and you learn to trim your own appetite. I admit, by that time, I was steadily learning what it means to have been "tired."

"Well, I see you clean up well, dearie," Elizabeth said after verbally and visually making sure that I had my hat, and scarf, and mittens, and no food on my shirt or rattles in my pockets. It was that kind of a cool blustery, more Winter, than Fall day.

Someone sat down beside me. Fresh. A little excess weight, elaborately dressed in something I couldn't quite characterize. Like a kaftan. Knit cap. I couldn't tell if it was slight makeup or just heightened facial coloring. The effect was like the raised circulation a brisk run in the cold gives. No jewels or bedecking. A strong scent, the kind that lingers in the clothes and furniture till the next day.

As a literal reminder.

I never asked the pronoun. We'll notice that in speaking to, the form is always "You" single or plural. And the proper form of self-address is "I," though people sometimes speak to themselves in second person.

As in, "You idiot."

I used to do that. To myself.

Until I realized this fragmentation was something like lowercasing the i. An irresponsible disassociation, and Tabitha chided me, to reel back in:

"In the original Greek, idiot means to be one's own person."

And then I embraced the Idiot. Mine and others.

"Hi. My name is Oli." Seats were close, by design, and I took up the awkwardly outstretched arm: "I'm trans."

It's an important thing to note here in perception. They teach now, in seminars on self-assertion, that whoever reaches out a hand first establishes dominance. I didn't make this condemnation.

To self or otherwise.

"Hi," I said back confidently, not feeling a need to identify myself. Impulse was to return to my papers, but something made me pause. I know what it was. It was the Invitation. Well, I had a minute— and an Exit. There were three people ahead of me in line. Oli had put out a calling card.

Figuratively speaking.

"How are you doing?" I continued taking the risk of opening one's self. To the unknown.

"I'm wonnnderful, thank you for asking. I'm new here. It's my first semester." Leaning in, for effect, but not disingenuously: "I'm a little Nnnervous."

"It doesn't show. I hope you like it here," I said.

"Haha! Thannk you. Do you?" dramatic emphasis. Wide open eyes suggestive of sincerity. I imagined in a minute or two that hand, drifting from cheek to thigh and back again, was going to land on my pantleg.

Some people are touchy feely. I brushed it off.

"Yes. Though, I'd like to think, I'd like it anywhere. So long as I could study. What are you majoring in? or are you still deciding what?" The black birds shattered the glass in the back of my mind. I pressed rewind and took a soundless inhale. Like Seamour taught me. To the diaphragm. It is after all *that* place that I finally went... Scholarship decided it. And maybe also the challenge. As if to face fears, head on.

"Gender Studies."

Oh, silent slow exhale. Of course.

"Interesting! What made you chose that area?" I said, trying not to sound all interview-like.

Certainly, I could begin to describe at this interval which way the transition apparently ran or speculate as to the resulting pronoun. But I won't.

I will point out that in the conversation that ensued it didn't matter.

I began to see the figure next to me as something like a Spirit— a Charles Dicken's abstraction of human past, present, and future. We always loved the concept of "Our Mutual Friend."

"Watching your world, through the charmed position of the dead Undead!" Seamour had exclaimed on slow reflection one particularly hot afternoon, us and Irving lolling on the grass beneath the Black Currant bushes secreted in the far shady corner of the north side garden.

Or at least, Elizabeth had remarked that these were near impossible to find in the States. Having been illegal. Something about Pepsin being rumored to be a critical component of Soda Pop. I looked that up. The ban on these berries was cited as due to a fungus, killing off the white pine. Northern coastal states reintroduced the bush very limitedly. Interesting, the Northeast coast is home to those endangered trees.

White pines have an eerie unreal silvery blue.

Oli continued. Eyes light, sparkling, speaking now with ease:

"Ever since I was little, I've had this strange sort of perception. Not ESP, or anything paranormal. I don't see auras, haha! It's just, I see every person in the fullness of fourth dimension. As 'They,' if you can understand."

I ducked my head, encouragingly, not yet sure.

The universe is said to be expanding, from a point smaller than the period at the end of our sentence.

I pictured a human egg. Roughly that size.

Smaller.

"...fragmenting," Oli continued, "Every person is a fraction of the species, and that piece is only half of the human experience. And we are baby, and child, and adult, and senior, and every phase in between. Our whole crowd of selves, in every instance, isolated in momentary snapshots in time. 'They.' Yet never to be complete, as 'human.' In that totality." The quotes, gesticulated.

"Because of sexes?" I asked, cautiously.

"Incomplete, yes, and looking for that other half, sometimes never finding a right puzzle piece... It's seldom a person is born with both the male and female, isn't it? It happens, and when it does it's treated like Jesus Christ. Everyone sees a baby that is a social threat, with a cross to bear, all deaf to 'love one another.'" Oli paused, especially:

"I feel lucky I could choose to make it happen."

"A holy experience?" I asked spontaneously, the visual and auditory pairing automatically rooting itself, in my mind, as hole and whole. The conversation itself struck me as otherworldly. Something like an observed out of body or near-death encounter. I remembered back to when Tabitha and I wondered about Phae, and again I had the distinctly creeping sensation…

That Oli was playing God. With awareness.

"It's like Chess. You can play against someone else, and that's a certain experience. You have a tentative alliance in the end, a partnership of opposition, friend or foe, you know? Or, go all in— you can play against yourself, and always win."

"Checkmated?"

Oli smiled: "Check."

We took a breath, simultaneously.

I felt the loss.

The finality of the word fuck closed on me. And I noticed Oli's ears were without lobe, connected directly to the skin at the jaw. Characteristic of a sociopath— I recalled reading somewhere.

I thought for an instant of parallel universes. How indirect "contact" with another is something I would not dismiss. Nor forfeit. Unique, distinctly separate. Mind to mind. Along side.

Like Tabitha. Seamour... Us.

"What are you studying?" Oli reciprocated politely with sincere interested expression even. I chided myself for that psychopath-sociopath thought. Though, sure enough, the hand went down. Ever so lightly, on my knee, and lifted. Unthreateningly. Oli suddenly seemed to me like a Religious. Having taken vows or orders. Not converting any-one, just appropriating, and testifying.

It occurred to me that Oli had strong will. A will to live. Maybe not generationally, but in this lifetime.

The secretary called, *"Next,"* and I rose.

"Theater and film," I said.

"Oh! Actor, or Director?"

"Documentarian. Art of the present, and Art of the past. I haven't thought out Art of the future yet," I said, smiling wryly, with a wave.

"Oh, alright thennn. Wow. Well, thannks! Bye!" affectation returning, on the decompress hiss, and emptying of my seat.

Maybe Oli was nervous.

18. the Crowd

Space is defined by people not metrics.

Sure, yeah by yourself, but if you haven't got sense of detachment up to Hindi snuff, then by other personalities that venture in (sometimes only in your mind). I've noticed for myself how my own personal confines change.

Alone, or with confidantes, I take up the whole room. Like we might be sitting in silence, and Seamour will say:

"Hey, quit hogging the space."

And I'll have to smile, sheepishly, because sure I knew they were there, on the other side of the kitchen or wherever. It was just really comfortable.

Seamour takes up the whole room too, but some how, we both fit. And it's better that way, I'd say— sharing. But other people come in, and the room shrinks like into a torturous cell.

A person doesn't even need to touch to be too close. You find yourself pulling in aspects of your self you didn't even realize were hanging out. When I do that I'm not even sure what those dang-lers are. Or why they're offending.

All I know is suddenly I feel lower case.

There's certain things I can, or can't, or won't.

Talking is one of them. Offering ideas is a close second. I like to think that I remain, in this reserve, helpful and polite. And I'd say I've come a long way in making space for others.

It was Walter who made me better recognize the socio-emotional dimensions of space. Walt was our mailman. It wasn't that there was any pushiness. Walt was our delivery man, but also manned the counter at the post office, depending on the day of the week. Or some other rotation in shifts that I never caught on to, otherwise I would have worked around the postal office employee schedule.

Like I would have aimed for the middle-aged working mom with the placid smile. Or better yet, the fragile old timer who over the years mastered presenteeism. As walking meditation. Ghosting through all the necessary motions, serenely, so that you felt reasonably freed of whatever your personal burdens— as if the guy had already one foot beyond, and we were all passing through.

But Walt had some kind of chip and was as if looking for flaws in others. Thing is, it wasn't stated. That heaviness. A feeling— overhead— of being judged.

Walter had, around the neck, a tie, as an emblem of authority. And it was shoved all the way aggressively. Self-punishingly. Everything, from facial expression, demeanor, carriage, dress, evoked resentment. For being here. For the work. For the fatigue. A grudge for living. Everything was, as if shorted. Like the shirt tails that refused to stay tucked, and Walt battled against, grunting and constantly poking a hand into overtight belt buckle just below the overhanging gut.

All, as you might imagine, accompanied by short temper.

If Walt kept the aggravation, the animosity, within the perimeters of self, it would have been one thing. (Inside.) Instead, you were drawn in. And I think most everybody resents being drawn in. Negativity is a vortex. Note how resentment seems to generate more and more of itself.

You see, Walt would go one or two steps short. A package delivered on the porch wouldn't be placed in the safety of the shade, nearest the door, with a polite tap-tap to let you know. No. It'd be left at the bottom of the stoop, exposed, where everyone could see it and pick it up, if having in mind theft.

A kind minded person would be proactive.

Not Walt.

And should you chance to catch the mail delivery in process, you could bet Walt would stand and wait for you to have to reach out for it, or even make you walk well out of your way. Now I would walk out to spare anyone, no big deal— that's my natural disposition— but I'm going to remind that the destination is the postal box, and the mailman isn't exactly put-out by going all the way there— though the other person could be considerate and catch the mailman half-way. Like I said, I would. Walt wouldn't.

Attitude is a fine attractant.

I knew Walt had a lonely life.

Again, it's that perpetuating cycle. Loneliness ensuring more loneliness, because Walt had embraced the empty idea of us "deserving it."

Whoever, or whatever, one might insert into the blank. That person, self or other, deserves their stinking lot.

It makes me sad to even think it.

In brief, Walter lived without love.

"Whatever we do," Seamour would say, "let's not do it without love." I took note of the specific twist, applied. The correct double negative. The thing didn't have to be affirmative. As in *with Love*. It merely needed to allow for Love, leaving a seat at the counter for the possibility. A presence.

Tabitha's wise, making that distinction, I think.

I approached the counter with my misgivings.

"Do you have anything to declare?"

"It's paper. Just paper."

"Media mail?"

*

Media. Now there's a word that conjures up a negative. For a moment I wanted to say, ugh, no! Conjuring images of porn and propaganda. And I had to reassure myself that not all media is "trash." I remembered just then that Sarah's a journalist. An investigative journalist.

In time, I learned the nature of the research. For Sarah it was a labor of familial love. In the broadest sense. I mean for Humanity. It was in those big files at the home office. I tried hard not to snoop, ever. I have this ingrained sense of Rights of Privacy. I suspect all private people do. By that I mean people who have worlds inside themselves. Not fantasy necessarily, but active stream of consciousness coupled with its own awareness.

Metacognition.

I'm pretty sure we all have this capacity, just not everybody is split up like that, to argue with themselves, or to subject their own person to interrogation, or to travel back mentally in time, or to invent alternate scenarios, or far-reaching fiction. It's probably why I didn't grill Tabitha when things got shady. For keeping a sense of security within your own reflections.

And for mental hygiene. People will share if they want to. Overshare even. Like I'd said, Seamour's sensitive, and moments of pause would be filled with depth. When ready.

With respect.

I never read Dad's journals. Never. Not even by accident, say, when doing chores.

And I've been used to doing household tasks. I see this as a vital responsibility, as Togetherness. It's right up there with Privacy for me. Taking care of the Earth or your corner of it no matter how little.

Woman's work it's called.

Which is pejoratively one step from servants' ...I'll notice there's also among those golden adages: *Cleanliness is next to Godliness.*

I took on vacuuming and yard work.

"I'll dust the old knickknacks," Sarah said kindly, meaning those tiny domestic treasures that are worth as much in sentiment as monetarily or not more so. These were things Sarah and Elizabeth had accumulated during work and travels, as well as heirloom pieces handed down to them from their parents and their grandparents.

Sarah cooked gourmet from scratch on most days and always did the dishes. Likewise, a collection of fancy inherited porcelain. Both agreed, and I'll concur that there's not much sense in saving finery for "one-day," when you can enjoy it and take care of it now. Sarah and Elizabeth were slow and deliberate in their thoughts and movements. Careful.

There was no hurry.

Elizabeth's gardening made its way to the pantry, as if on schedule (its own, of course). And I only needed to assist on high branches for pruning or deep recesses of the gutters, because Elizabeth shooed me, lightly:

"Don't be taking my work from me, dearie. What will I do with myself if you go pulling up all the weeds, folding all the laundry, and takeover the baking? And, anyway, I'm very particular. But, I promise, I'll give you as many tips as you like if you'd just keep me company in the yard or the kitchen."

And it wasn't that I was prohibited from the office, or the attic, or any room. My family home was our house now— Our home even. No sense of devious secrecies, or suspicious separations.

So, it happened like this. I was vacuuming. I was thinking about what Seamour said years ago, that at the moment of the Big Bang an equal portion of antimatter should have been generated, along with the matter that we can see.

Micro and macro scopic.

That kind of blew my mind.

"Has anyone 'found' antimatter?"

"Apparently its known by effect, and adjacent findings. Electrons have their opposites."

"Really?"

"Positrons."

I wasn't sure what to make of this info.

"Particles have like these mirror selves, seemingly identical, except in charge."

"And what happens when they meet?"

"Annihilation."

Seamour explained that the understanding is that there cannot be the same amount of antimatter loose in the Universe, or it would all self-destruct. It's somehow locked up. And when the known matter-anti-matter collides, light is emitted.

"Huh." I said, thinking about lightning, and static sparks, and electricity in general. I suspected, too, that when the light is emitted, not all the matter is spent. So, annihilation is the maybe wrong word.

There's like leftovers hence disproportionate ratio of something to nothing.

Honestly, it made me think, on a tangent, that there are few eggs to sperm. That matter and anti-matter is something like sexual tension.

It exists, in potentiate.

Occasionally something sparks.

I was going round the high back chairs with the swivel attachment of the Eureka canister. Suddenly, whoooosh. Vrrrr... Ffflll, something stuck to the surface. Flat. It was a thick piece of paper. Glossy on the underside. I knew Sarah had been busy unpacking some lingering boxes from the move.

Dad's room became my room. It was just, we agreed, and the two guest bedrooms were picked between Sarah and Elizabeth. One adjacent to the library, which also served as the office, upstairs. The other on the ground floor, Northeast, nearest the kitchen, facing the garden. My new room was to the West, with a small balcony. That side of the main floor was over the partially buried garage and basement. My old room was now the new guest room. And that way we all had "moved."

In the Library, I had not *all* our old books, but most. And some very important papers. Like the deed to the house, adoption forms, Irving's veterinary records, medical papers, Dad's death certificate. And most invaluable, in my eyes, were our few family pictures.

Sarah, Elizabeth and I spent a rainy weekend pouring over these. Everything looking archaic. The house, the neighborhood. Unnamed elders. Baby Irv. Me, and Tabitha. An elaborate yellowing white wedding album. Documentation, Dad had said grimly. And I would never have thrown it out, anyway.

"We have some photos."

"Some! Now that's an understatement. We have so many pictures and not even in protective sleeves like these. Oh, we'll have to dig those up and preserve them nicely like this. Our mother had them boxed so many years. Nobody had time to set them out properly into albums. Fortunately, we have them well taped up," said Elizabeth.

Apparently, Sarah had dug those out finally. On leaning up, I could see there were a couple stacks on the desk. Several boxes under. I turned the floor attachment upside down, then shut the vac, and flipped the thing over. The photo fluttered into my palm. Now right-side up.

It was black and white.

It was a silver haired black woman, flanked by two small light skinned children. On the back in precise script handwriting it read *Grandmama*. I speculated the two cute toddlers were Sarah and Elizabeth.

They didn't look colored.

On reflection, Elizabeth's halo may very well have gotten its beautiful volume naturally, by genetics. I assumed it was permed. Or curled so, from years of dyes. Sarah's earthy skin, now struck me as mocha, rather than sun tanned.

I didn't need to ask. When they came in from the midday walk in the yard, they were very excited.

"Do you have a moment?" Sarah asked.

"We just pulled out those boxes we were talking about, a month or so ago, from storage. You know, the old, sealed family photos! Very old, saved on from our great great grandmother Elwynn, dearie. We can't wait to show you!!"

Grandmama Elwynn, it turned out, was the only partly African American pictured. Darker in the photo, Sarah said. And dilute continued in the next generation, and the next, with subsequent marriages. Greenish gray eyes, in rich skin tone. A slight frizz to the hair. Even eventually as light as Elizabeth's.

"Genes get passed unpredictably," Sarah noted, and I pondered about nature versus nurture.

Chromosomes. I thought of Seamour.

Other expecting parents carry around *The Healthy Pregnancy Guide* or *What to Name the Baby,* I was carrying *X: A Fabulous Child's Story*. A very thin book, with wood block like illustration in the classic colors reminiscent of WWII. Red, Black, and a flesh color, nearing yellow. Sallow.

Sarah and Elizabeth gave it to me, and I received it with a combined fascination and horror. I won't deny it had me thinking back to Phae, wondering, what happened to them?

What I could say, unequivocally, was that as the years passed, there was more "Them."

There is no typographical error, above.

To be clear, I want to point that out to readers and publishers. Lest anyone be tempted to insist on a correction, or on the insertion of a [sic] notation.

I mean exactly that— more people were using this form of reference. Them.

There wasn't more "of them."

There was more "Them." You'll notice things were very much in that steady flux of what everchanging nomenclature has dubbed as "Normalization."

My Moms didn't blink at our opting for the They pronoun prior.

It was Elizabeth actually who introduced me to Dąbrowski's ideas of Positive Disintegration. We were pruning the hedges in our back yard. The ones Dad had planted with very strict instructions that the blossoms must be cut after wilting. Deadheading it's called. Else the plant proliferate like an alien invasion. I forget sometimes what the plant is called. I think I've mentioned it before.

We think the flower head decays and is simply taken into the ground, but these heads don't disintegrate like petals and leaves. They take root. The idea of positive disintegration is that tension and its release, like stress and its resolution, build a more autonomous person, over time. Not just an individual.

One who is not easily swayed or uprooted.

X is a child whose parents have agreed to keep and raise entirely pronoun-less, not even as "they." The agreement further necessitated that X would be treated gender neutrally. X would play dolls and football. X would dress in sexless garb. X would remain, for as long as possible, unaware of being male or female.

I'll admit it had certain philosophical appeal as potentially philanthropic. Loving people.

Except. Except.

The keeping of, from, bothered.

You know.

Knowledge.

It had me suddenly thinking all Biblical. What troubles is that which was known would be obscured supposedly as a protective shielding from...

I imagined that child as Pissed Off.

Like finding out you were adopted. Or have some genetic condition. None of these "bad" in or of themselves, but a rational person wants to know. Regardless. We come to terms, with whatever. We have to. But lack will shape a person with a certain dent, I imagine.

It's been suggested that the first chapter of the Bible is so different from the rest of the Old

Testament that it seems to have been written by some other hand.

Genesis.

When all was Good. Presumably through to *the end*.

That moment. You know: When They Knew.

19. the Hospital

"I think it was when you found out about forced sterilizations, wasn't it?" Elizabeth asked Sarah.

That was the nature of the research. Sarah and Elizabeth's family had been very poor, and wedlock hadn't sanctified the children born to Grandmama. There was a lot of pressure at the time over reproductive rights but not the kind you might think.

Seamour never mentioned it.

We had discussed it, in abstraction, like we discussed God. Well back, as children.

"I imagine I wouldn't abort no matter what."

And I really did think Tabitha could stand by that statement. The *even-if's?* drifted to mind, silently. I wanted to believe that as a mother I would also be that strong. Rape, disability, or illness.

All as untestable hypothetical.

Integrity of personhood seems paramount. By which I mean, a person *live* with their decision.

Sarah was tight lipped as ever: "I'll show you some articles, if you like."

Elizabeth pressed on, "It was a gross push from social organizations, with insidious, potentially government policy implications, to encourage low-income people to undergo operations or otherwise get on birth control. It was even argued people born with disabilities should be required to undergo vasectomies or hysterectomies or tubal litigations!"

Sarah's research went further. It explored the plight of those born intersex and being subject to gender normalizing surgeries without ability to consent.

Children.

I read the articles, and the critiques. The info was presented candidly. The dissent was that the topic was breached at all. The theme of Eugenics made people very uncomfortable, horrified even, as much as Xenophobia. We want to believe the impulse to modify mankind has gone with WWII. Or that it was somehow contained scientifically in the purview of PhDs, or regulated "business," where "nature," not-people, were concerned... Seems over the years genetic experiments became very quiet, whether plant or animal. Bureaucratic. Post genetically modified corn... And seal of company patents.

Out of the scope of individuals, as if.

One of Sarah's articles gave a warning that some things become very ordinary over time. Like male circumcision. And it takes the publicizing of the "unheard of" female genital mutilation to make people cry out— Hey! there's a problem.

A human problem.

It was a difficult subject and I admired Sarah for the years spent in what must have been thankless trenches. People should know. And think on it.

We lip, "knowledge is power."

It may seem curious, but Tabitha and I were never concerned about the Other. Not *each other,* but as in that vague Antigen. The foreigner. The unknown. Every generation maybe has its own slant in its view of existence. For ourselves, I note it was never "Us against Them." If we had a paranoia, it was over falling into some labeled compartmental drawer. Especially one we didn't cosign.

Guess that's why the proactive taking control of...

If I had to explain it would be like the phenomenon of Opting Out. It was natural to us, the status quo.

...As we were growing up, the rules had changed.

Holdan had pointed it out in passing. Junk mail had arrived. Same old, same old seemingly, but suddenly it got the "goat."

One would never think to hear the phrase, *back in the day* from Holdan, yet there it lingered in the air:

"Used to be you had to Opt In. You had to be in the know. You had to make an effort. You had to go. Demonstrate adroitness over hoops and hurdles. You had to give name and address and bank number to validate yourself as accounted."

Uphill both ways, Holdan...

...Now you had to make an effort to extract yourself out of a quarry from hands that would data mine you down to your last byte. For free. Gratis.

Nonbinary, as it turned out is something of a feeling, rather than any observable fact. Like astrology is to astronomy. Or intuition to instinct, maybe. When Phae had first dropped the term on us, like I said, we thought in regard to the physical.

Maybe that's why things took the turn they did, as we screwed our selves into the dressing of things, from names to clothes, till hitting the brick shit ton of processes. The fan blade if you will.

The way things actually work.

Identification. Like a tag on a body bag.

In our last years of high school we had a heroin crisis. That's what we were told— kids were overdosing. What we saw was the crackdown: Police, drug sniffing canines, and the installation of metal body scanners at the main doors. And we had to have at all times, like a dog tag, our school ID strapped around our necks.

Name, photo, and QR-code.

The chorus in the halls in lieu of Hi and How you doing was: "Badge? Badge? Hey! do you have your ID badge. Let me see your badge."

As part of some last dash citizen awareness, we were required to take a Government class in our final year, before graduation. You know as requisite. We had a special instructor come in, an adjunct from one of the nearby colleges, to help also push *that* idea (of Continuing Education). It was when Seamour was missing a lot of school. I remember being alone that day. The instructor was a Cynthia Somebody but had said casually that we could all use the informal "Cindy." Like we were on par when we know teachers and students never are.

It made us uncomfortable in those late years. Kind of like "Phae," but more so. Most opted then for no form of addressee, or Miss, which probably offended oddly. You see, Cynthia, whose family name thanks to the disregard has effectively escaped my long term, wanted so hard to still be "young." You know, one of us. The class raised eyebrows. Some kissed up, sensing weakness. Vanity. It's hard to pin-point, so many little things that add and don't add up. It's like seeing a female drag queen. Excess. Lack of confidence, and it evoked a kind of leering pity.

Too much lipstick.

At one point our lack luster engagement in the lecture broke the ole camel's back, for no real reason. Cynthia, who had from the beginning brought in a college style podium (a lectern I think it's called), gave a little smack down of a tightly clenched fist on its shiny wooden surface. Like a gavel. Sending the prepared papers jumping, but not yet scattering. Cynthia wanted something from us, but we weren't sure what.

With excessive pause, and woeful outgrown pout, Cynthia declared, "I am not going to stand up here and dance for you all," and then angrily contained the yellow legal ruled pad with old fashioned blue cursive handwriting in one manicured hand, while hoisting a large purse from beside the podium. Then click-clacked out the door. Tight jeans and six-inch stiletto boots hampering the walk, as Cythnia used the paper occupied hand to wrap a fluffy white muffler elaborately around the neck. Hoop earrings and jeans jacket collar further offending the effort.

Privately, I'll bet we each thought a mature person with self-regard wouldn't come back after such exposition— on reflection. And can school staff just walk out like that? We had about ten minutes to the dismissal bell.

But we were like dogs, beaten.

Cynthia did come back, the next day, even more platinum blonde, and we redoubled our efforts in unenthusiastic obedience to earn that pending class participation grade. Learning about Law.

Seamour speculated, later, on hearing about it, that maybe the instructor was on the rag?

Only they would know.

For some reason, nonbinary sounds to me like nonbinding. Something like a legal contract.

Actually, nonbinary I found means not identifying with one gender or another, or both, or neither... And it had nothing to do with what equipment biologically you got or whether even you opted for sex change.

I finally understood it was after all a garment, washable, dryable, ironable, mendable, and alterable. Something like a mental shawl, and as such its role was to cloak and comfort. Provide warmth, or shield from damaging rays. Not UV, but something like that... with a questioning of what we'd call "ethics."

Turns out "Of Mice and Men" is a title also inspired by Burns. The poem, "To a Mouse."

"Jenny?
...Adamov?"

It was the hospital chaplain as startled at me as I.

I guess I'd been in closed circuit. It had been a while since anyone was surprised. I turned around with stubble from several days, and tucked my hair behind an ear, and smoothed the pleats of the skirt Seamour had picked from Goodwill only a couple months ago.

It occurred to me that I might look like a hobo. Someone fallen on their luck, throwing on whatever they got to shield from the weather. Finding oneself here after having walked a long time, in crisis. I imagined I looked old. Shriveled, something like the witch from Snow White. About to go vile.

The chaplain in customary black clerical uniform held out a delicately aged palm to shake: "I'm here for bereavement support, if you need."

I shook.

I hadn't had any, ever, not even when Dad died. The pit of my stomach tanked. I wondered what it felt like to have carried a child. How precious and in-tuned. I had tried consciously not to envy Seamour that special connection I knew was forming. That unique physical intimacy.

I pictured it tied like the umbilical cord. Though that aspect I suppose was mostly wireless. And then maybe, I too tapped in, ear to belly. All those silent conversations we had. Sometimes I felt so much like an insider that I was also in utero.

Tabitha carrying the lot of us.

"The chapel is out here to the left. Right around that corner. You can press the silver button on the wall if you should like to have someone come to talk or just to sit with you," soft smile in sympathy.

"It's a challenging pregnancy."

Squeezing my fingers, covering one hand with the other, and letting go, when I lost my words and only nodded slowly in acknowledgement.

The Chaplain added:

"Doesn't have to be to pray, so's you know, but that too. If you like," kindly.

Then, realization. The terrible fear that the little one would not make it. Would never see the world, or be seen, or known, and Seamour was adamant about not knowing if Cherub were boy or girl.

"We're all nonbinary in thought," Seamour says, having looked it up eons ago.

"Then why all the hubbub?" I had asked Cherub telepathically. The unborn didn't exactly answer, but the silence was telling.

When I first found out, my subsequent gasp was for the possibility of multiples. "What if it's twins?" I said stupidly.

Cherubim.

"Definitely octuplets," Tabitha answered drily, eyes closed darkly, hospital sheets pulled up under the chin. Obviously, I wasn't helping.

I snuck a kiss on the nose, standing up to creep out. "Bathroom," I said softly hearing the ruffle of protest.

Which one did I use? The closest one. And I had tears in my eyes. I didn't see what the icon was... I ran to the nearest stall and did the unisex thing.

I threw up.

I remembered watching Repulsion on dvd with Tabitha. I mean, I watched Seamour's face. Seamour explained later disgust for Catherine Deneuve. For looks? I asked, intrigued, as I thought we were beyond that. Apparently, it had something to do with the roles the star took on.

Then, I understood: Deneuve played women.

"Ugly women," said Seamour.

Ugly on the inside. Grotesquely otherwise attract-ive symmetrical females, in face and figure, who thought every male wanted a chance at the snatch or could be led by the nose or dangling carrot to work overtime for the trophy.

Sarah and Elizabeth were plain, absolutely. There was nothing in their features that suggested they'd ever been lookers. In the cheap sense of the word. They took care of themselves. Without pretension. Without revisionist lack of esteem, which I'd say cosmetics and adornments tend to suggest. (Incidentally, Tabitha's hair and face was never painted, either.) They both had a sparkle that a good spirit gives every body it inhabits. Each in their own way.

I reconsidered my own brash judgement.

What is plain?

There was after all something about each of them, physically, that *was* beautiful. Sarah's translucent olive skin while aged with thinness and delicate blue purple veins, had the finesse of fine vellum. Elizabeth's hair was a crowning halo. The gentle character of their voices gave a sense of integrity and calm, and distinctive humor that added to conversations an ease and intelligence.

Seamour said, in other parts of the world, it happens all the time.

Holdan had taken them a few times out of country. Short two or three days out. Tabitha sent beautiful postcards. Something about knowing that the borders-of-the-world don't end on Hollywood, prompted those trips. Apparently across the world nobody thinks much of it. Even towards the Mediterranean and East. Like Turkey.

Two women. Two men. Walking arm in arm.

Just walking. For goodness sake. I mean conversing, listening, observing. Enjoying each other's damned company. Bathing even—but that's not what I'm getting at here, except to say that it means a lot, and very little.

The togetherness.

I guess I felt a lingering guilt. The thought had after all crossed my own polluted mind like a maligned black cat. Remember, back when I first met Sarah and Elizabeth? What was it I had stupidly said about their "relationship?" Pathetic speculation.

They were people.

First and foremost. Good people. They put others before themselves. I cannot understand the violence that overcomes some individuals against others. What's even, rightly said, as "none of their business."

What are haters (of anything) so afraid of?

Then again, I think to myself, it's more than that. Mankind has this impulse against procreation. To separate and limit. To apply pesticide.

I remember being in fourth grade, with several of the neighborhood children, slightly older. I'd found a snake. Or so I thought.

Someone shrieked. It was actually two Gardners, connected grotesquely, facing opposite. (Not Ouroboros like.) One of the girls grabbed a thick stick and making yucking noises, shook them apart till the two forcibly separated and scattered, and somebody shouted: *"Fuck!"*

It was only later that I knew they were copulating.

Those snakes at least garnered some respect. Not like houseflies or mosquitoes, who are summarily slapped under bare hand for the natural mating transgression. Interestingly, I had an old friend, three times my age, Sigmund, no kidding, who said that that was the way to go. Making love in nature and having a tree fall on you.

"I don't see the attraction," said Tabitha.

I imagine it's the after image that bothers, but that's the compromise. And you're not really there to see the clean up anyway. Or if you are, and maybe you go and laugh over it— it's not on your conscience anymore.

My long-winded point is, given all this hate, we might very well think this a fine solution. Presto. Ineffectual pairings. Thanks be to god for all non-heterosexuals.

But, no.

I didn't acknowledge the significance though, of hate, even with all these peripheral contemplations. Sarah and Elizabeth went out of the house very moderately. Outings driven by necessity—a trip to the post office or the supermarket, some research at the library, the weekly worship at their church. Many times they went out separately, because they kept busy. Sarah, retired or no, put in a lot of time in our library office reading and writing. Elizabeth tended the garden and baked. They liked spending time at home, both alone and together.

What I'm saying is that I never feared for them.

And having adopted them, I should have. I should have been more mindful. I know now. A parental instinct should have kicked in. No different than when drawing in (to your heart) a cat or a dog or a hamster. A child. And we are all children.

Vulnerable, I mean.

I've learned since that it's something like taking a toddler out for a special occasion. Everything gets shifted out of routine and decision making becomes irregular and more impromptu. Risk increases. Happy delirium. That gnawing feeling that everything is peachy and all the world must be good.

That's when it happens.

Evil.

It may very well be that I had only thought of myself. Wanting to give Sarah and Elizabeth a "day out." Ugh, not that I wanted to do something nefarious. I wanted, undoubtedly, that elevated feeling that comes along when you think you are doing a kindness. Yet, haven't actually thought, through to the end in full. Resulting in that obnoxious protest, *"but I only wanted to…"*

It was Holdan that answered my call. Holdan who said simply:

"We don't foresee these things," suggesting that a well-disposed mind thinks in terms of greater goods. Not lesser evils. I already had Tabitha in and out of the hospital with precarious pregnancy. That should have put me more on guard. Seamour would have been wiser. Advocated against going out, this time. Tabitha would have said adding to happiness makes it overflow, and then? — Disaster.

Sarah and Elizabeth, through all of this, had not blamed or chided or been anything other than supportive. No stern talk of being responsible, or failing to think of the future… Tabitha's, mine, others. I secretly suspected they were downright pleased at the turn of events… their childlessness remedied two or three-fold, maybe more. They liked Seamour, of course, like a two-fer for starters, seeing at once, that Tabitha was fundamental to me.

There was no mistake in their eyes.

But I made an error. Of judgement.

It was Friday afternoon, a day out from school. I'd just gotten my driver's license. It was delayed in happening, and so all the more special. And I thought, elated, *my treat*—

"Let me take you to The Cream Carousel!" I declared magnanimously.

If you're not familiar, The Cream Carousel is the bestest ice cream place. It has as if every variety, dairy and nondairy, but better yet, it has a beautiful ride. The vintage kind with wooden horses and a lion and elephant, as well as several fancy bench seats. In its center, a genuine band organ machine. Wind-bellows below blowing air into metal pipes. People of all ages can get on the carousel and feel secure. A baby in your arms could relax and smile contentedly on that CC ride.

The unit's finagled so that it's indoors outdoors. A glass roof and side panels stay up for winter, and then the walls are removed from the frame during summer. The roof stays, for all the time use, rain or shine. And it doesn't ever have the sadness of places that stick out that sorry sign:

[Closed for the Season.]

I'd never seen happier wrinkles. Elizabeth and Sarah grasped each other's hands, beaming like little sisters, and giggling delightedly. They were already pleased that I'd passed. And of course, they wanted to celebrate with my first "legal" victory lap. Sarah went in to get those hiking sandals that I had said were practical and cute, and Elizabeth ran out back to look for a favorite sun bonnet.

The important thing is that the place was on the far side of town. Where none of us went much. I hadn't been to the CC in ages. Last time I'd went it was somebody's birthday party in elementary.

In addition to the ride, as an attraction, the place was across the street from a public park. It was Elizabeth that got the idea. After a brief consultation with Sarah and much smiling and patting of my hand, Elizabeth said:

"Dearie, why don't you go along home? We'll walk in the park a bit and take the bus. I see the stop is right there at the end of this sidewalk and we're not in any hurry, are we? Then you can feel like you had the car to yourself."

Well, fact was, if I was driving with Sarah and Elizabeth, it was just like being on permit. It was generous, frivolous, and just like Elizabeth to forget that there're Dutch windmill cookies that needed to be baked for the church social on Saturday and other small tasks that needed attending. Sarah held their cones. Elizabeth re-tied the bonnet as we made our way out.

I grinned, "Well, yeah that would be awesome. But I know you don't actually have a lot of time, and we don't know the bus schedule here. Maybe I'll just drive around for a bit, explore, and pick you up in a half hour?"

It seemed so damn reasonable. They each gave my hand another squeeze and turned down the pathway into the park, walking arm in arm, amiably. Elizabeth leaning in close to Sarah's ear. Both were losing their hearing a little bit.

I thought they looked lovely. Picturesque. Two elegant ladies.

As I turned, I drew my hair back, and from under its curtain saw a group of kids staring. I was pretty used to it, I guess. Blasé. From this perspective, I don't even remember what I was wearing. The stare was the standard question, "what is it?" and I'd come to dismiss this peering— in regard to my person. Boy or Girl? was the question that hovered. Seymour and I had cultivated if I may say, something like a non-androgynous cross.

Still, requiring a double take. You see how I only limitedly thought of myself. Ashamedly.

I tucked the dismissal of the groupies into my gray cells and got into the red Acura.

Sarah was very proud, with their father having been a lifelong car mechanic, to have some knowledge about what was what in the auto world. Acura I soon learned is the premium brand affiliated with Honda. Like Lexis, with Toyota. It was a nice car. I could feel the staring eyes on me, from the point of departure with Elizabeth and Sarah, to the keyless opening of the car. And then relief. That sense of security, on closing the insulated door.

Vacuum packed. A safe shell.

Maybe if I didn't have that antagonizing run-in on my way to the library still lingering in the back of my head, I would have been less self-absorbed. Maybe not. The thing is I didn't think at all about Sarah and Elizabeth. No, of course, I turned my head to check on them and give a final wave, should they glance back. They didn't, actually—and that wasn't it.

It's not that I didn't think about them.

I didn't think of their safety.

I wasn't really sure where to go. This beautiful gifted ride was totally unexpected, and no other particular destination was known to me around here. I had determined to give the two about fifteen minutes of strolling. I'd drive around a bit, fill the tank, find a parking spot and start looking out for them. Not more than half an hour, max.

It ought to have tipped my concern when I looked in the rearview and saw the group of starers peel from the low wall that held flowers and tall ornamental grasses. They had moved together, a step or two towards my direction, but as I checked the mirror again, in traffic, the herd of malcontents was shifting into the park.

Some minds are disposed to think Negative.

I didn't want to be that person. Or maybe, I just wasn't. They were curious, that's all, I told myself. I can clearly remember a time when I thought I saw someone I recognized from a distance. I was so intent on looking and checking. And re-checking. I completely disregarded how that looked from the other side. It wasn't intentional. I just couldn't see well in the glare of the sun. But I needed to know. It was someone I hadn't seen in years.

I don't even want to go into that story.

You look at somebody like that and something will happen. It did. I got a black eye. I was 16. It scared the wits out of my Moms. I had thought it was Raymond. It looked like Raymond, but with prosthetic leg. I stared and stared, and worse, I got closer. By the time I was close enough to be sure it wasn't, Non-Raymond took several brisk strides forward and socked me. I guess it was the ski cap. The relative height or something about the figure in general. Proportions. Or maybe, it was power of suggestion which then, in not adding up, had transfixed me to the spot. Till I was like, "What the hell, man?!"

In retrospect, I deserved that. I could have used my words. Before the punch. My moms thought it was my first fight. I wanted to say it was somebody trying to steal my bike, for lack of reasonable explanation. But I humbled myself and described it as it was, and they were relieved. An accident of sorts. This was after the grim Library incident. And yeah, I know I should've been more considerate. Remembering how they'd worried about my physical person.

The light turned green.

I turned left into a street filled with pleasant shops. Antique places, an eyeglass store, a craft and frame shop, a couple of jewelers, and a hot tacos and shots eatery. Then I spotted a bookstore, and an empty parking spot. It called out to me. That parallel parking spot. I eased into it like a pro, with no nerves. No intimidation. It was no longer a test—I could drive! Felt almost as good as fly. Elizabeth was right. It was thrilling this first moment on my own with the vehicle. The bookstore wasn't one of those big box snob places that vend freshly minted works, which publishers have placed their bets on like horses at the races. It was old, and every book in it was older.

At first I had that pang, that I should bring some one here, like Seamour, or Sarah and Elizabeth. Holdan even. But here I am, and I've time to kill, so I should scout it out on my own. I hadn't lost my head, completely. I set my phone to give an alarm in ten minutes, proactively. You know this is the kind of place that is a time warp. It sucks you in and before you know it, two hours are gone.

Fiction or nonfiction.

Sure enough, I'd swear I had been all of two minutes, when the beep, beeping started. I'd just gotten a hold on a boxed clothbound "Revolt of the Angels," by Anatole France. A beautiful hardcover with illustrations. If you don't know the story, it features a disgruntled guardian Archangel who reads some philosophical texts in their charge's library and (based on those human ideas) plots a rebellion against God... and nothing comes of it... surprise, surprise, everything remains as is... in its constant existential struggle. To the human mind.

I bought the book and felt reinforced in the great successes of the day. I didn't hurry much because I was well within that roughly slated half-hour max. I was just a couple minutes, by car, from the park. Midday traffic was minimal.

I looked with excitement across the walkways to spot my Moms. The park was flat. Easy visibility mostly. Except it had a concert proscenium. With steps that also served as seats. I parked and continued to scan the pathways. Nothing. I paused and covered my eyes from the sun to better check around the intermittent trees, and small groupings of people. Anxiety crept in. I worked my way towards that proscenium.

If you're imagining those raised stages, that's not it. This dipped down, as a bowl for acoustics. I couldn't see in all the way, till I got closer to the edge. There was Sarah at the bottom with her arm around Elizabeth, who was doubled over. They'd gotten tired I'd thought, seeing them seated. My chest tight.

Doubt said: that is not like them. I quickened my pace. Sarah turned as soon as my footsteps echoed towards them across the concrete stairs. Concern behind the glasses.

Then I could see Elizabeth was hurt.

"My foot, dear. It'll be ok." So few words told me it was not okay. Elizabeth, with a brave face, was also holding a hand, awkwardly, over the right shoulder. Right hand holding the ankle.

"We need to hobble Lizzie out of here," said Sarah.

My instant imagining—of Sarah and Elizabeth toppling over together, again down the stairs as I tried and failed to crutch Elizabeth's foot, which was probably sprained, up the massive stairs— prompted me to call Holdan.

While we waited Sarah explained exactly what happened. It was hard for Elizabeth to talk more than a word or two, accompanied by what was best described as a small pleasant grimace. I had to fill in some missing pieces. But I gathered that the group of punks that had eyed me, had put together that I was with Elizabeth and Sarah. For reasons not quite fathomable, they'd pursued the two.

"This is the rock," said Sarah holding up a heavy gray stone the size of a tennis ball. Not exactly round. I took hold of it. It was only somewhat lighter than it initially looked because one side was rounded and the other was jagged.

One of the starers had grabbed it and on getting close had chucked it. Assholes. It struck Elizabeth in the right shoulder and because the two were walking along the edge admiring the proscenium, arm in arm still, or so I imagined, they'd lost balance. Sarah, as the smaller and sprightlier of the two, recovered, having the added advantage of being on the left. While Elizabeth, with surprise of impact, and pain, had teetered over the edge. The right ankle had taken first impact as well as a rolling-over, down several steps, before Sarah was able to scramble out in front of Elizabeth to block further tumbling.

"We hobbled down the next few steps to sit down for a minute."

I'm not sure what they thought. They didn't seem scared. I sat between them and told them about my drive, as distraction. It took sixteen minutes for Holdan to arrive. Fast, all considering. Holdan and I took Elizabeth under each arm and five legged we made it up the ten steps. Then I hurried back to lend an arm to Sarah.

"Sprains don't swell immediately," Holdan said, when Elizabeth started objecting to going to the urgent care clinic.

"We're going," I said, and with a grateful wave to Holdan, I rolled up the window and drove us there. The bruise on the shoulder also needed to be examined. It occurred to me that no one had told Holdan about the rock. Only that Elizabeth had fallen and that it was too dangerous for one person, or me and Sarah, to try to navigate Elizabeth up the concrete step seats. Had it been Sarah that fell, Elizabeth and I might have been able to manage without help. Holdan didn't see the situation as upsettingly as I did. Probably, my Moms didn't either.

I saw it as a Hate Crime. Maybe I am the radical.

It made me angry.

Moreso, it made me sad.

I couldn't bring myself to tell Tabitha. I had nightmares about everyone being in the hospital. Everyone that I cared most about. Tabitha, Sarah, Elizabeth, Holdan, my Dad. When I woke up my jaw hurt.

I must've been grinding my teeth or something.

Brykein.

Greek, for that wretched refrain in the scriptures, the Old Testament, referred to as the "wailing and gnashing of teeth."

The poetic anguish of the wicked.

It was on that trip to the Emergency Room that I saw Zeke.

20. Miscarriage

For my 10th birthday, Dad gave me a book called "Logic and Language." Needless to say, it took a long while for teething. I was 17 when I finally sunk my chomps in, and a bit more for digesting it. The part that really stood out to me was the summary on misleading expressions. The professor, in essay, called to our mind the "null and void" presented by the carnivorous-cow, as an example... and then pondered the logic of the phrases *God exists,* as well as *Satan does not exist*. And the reversal of both assertions. The ponderance being that *unlike the I in my state-ment 'I am hungry,'* says the author, there may or may not be an actual entity in those previous two statements. Then again, the I in the sample also may only exist as "idea." Yet not as a falsehood. Some point must be true. Nobody really being hungry. And everyone being hungry at some time.

Hence the disconnect.

I mean the mislead.

It charmed Tabitha to no end, the point about the grain of truth being that the "Noise" exists. You know, as in the very articulation itself. Vocalized or internalized.

A babble.

"Regardless of the word," Tabitha mused then with a slight shake of the head. Because we, as humans, will assume the meaning, whatever the sound. Like that fundamental utterance, in regard to self—

—I. Or whatever stand-in.

And billions and billions of definitions. That also need to accept that, that "I," exists.

.

I touched Tabitha's hair softly. My hand clutched to the chest, the heart really. The other hand, left, extended anemically.

"Are we going to make it?"

"Yeah," I said gently, taking those cold limp fingers between the heat of my palms. The EKG weak.

If Life teaches anything it's to leave the dying Hope.

I pressed my lips to those tips and tried to hide my tears. The doctor said the uterus did not contract correctly. Causing uncontrolled hemorrhaging.

Hospitals have been sanitized, professionally, in every way from evasive stock answers to outfits. Nurses' uniforms wiped from matronly dresses to unisex "scrubs," and the room temperatures made as cold as the legs of a frigid wife. Harsh bright examination lights bored down for soul searching examination. Everything as if to short comfort.

Neutralizing.

Made me think of Walt.

Even schoolteachers nowadays have permission to mitigate the glare of fluorescents by covering the overhead bulbs with clip-on nylon flag-like sheets set in place across the ceiling by magnets to the metal frame of the outer light panels. Sometimes solid colored, sometimes cosmic pattern or passing clouds. The thinness of the fabric lets light filter through more gently.

Suddenly I was rereading about Jenny Fields. In the hospital. The way Jenny had essentially raped a dying mostly brain-dead bed-ridden soldier to conceive a child. A son. The idea being to avoid the interpersonal exchange, beyond bodily fluid. The compromise that social relation requires.

God bless it wasn't a daughter. Just saying.

Why is that important? Why, when I've spent all these words to say it shouldn't matter. Like there's this permanent display, a large, framed piece of bright Graphic Art— big, shiny, set behind Plexi-— in the hospital waiting area. To similar effect.

It reads in multicolor:

***

We Welcome...

All Races and Ethnicities
All Religions
All Spoken Languages
All Gender Identities
All Sexual Orientations
All Abilities
All Ages
All Sizes
All Education and Income levels
All Insured and Uninsured

***

Because it's not enough to say, "All People."

.

My Moms fell silent. I pulled the Acura into the parking lot nearest the Emergency entrance, and we could see a small ambulance approaching. Entering traffic, the siren blared a short warning blast. I had that defined contrast. The hurry and the delay. Sarah and I worked together to help Elizabeth out from the front passenger seat in slow motion, against that backdrop of emergency. We approached the curb. Crossed the crosswalk. Scaled the curb opposite. All the while, the lit ambulance struggled for time.

Whosoever was in there was apparently in need of life support. There were five people on the crew. Each bustling. Strapping straps. Lifting and lowering the stretcher, unlocking the wheels. Communicating by radio:

"Incoming. Critical."

"Roger. Left entrance, ER R 102. Stats?"

"Female. 13 or 14. Evangeline Shaw."

"Roger."

"ICD-10 956. Carpo."

"Roger. Left or Right?"

"Both."

"Roger."

I suppose now I'll be criticized for inconsistency. Worse. Hypocrisy. But all the info in this very tense scenario— name, along with the details of age and life-threatening injury— had conjured up a *girl*.

I can't explain well. The mental picture is generic. That certain softness of cheek, or jaw, relation of eye to eyebrow to nose to chin. Big or small. Thin or fat.

Pretty or plain.

What rolled out of the ambulance was sexless.

Gaunt. Young, but ageless. Fragile. Pale. More naked than naked, though covered mostly by white sheet. Thin arms were heavy over the cloth. Both wrists strapped down and swathed in gauze. Applied thick and tight, so as not to bleed through. It was like a victim of war.

It was then that it hit me. Wordlessly. It was as if I knew. Fundamentally.

This one had made the ultimate rejection.

Neither, nor.

The face was near lifeless, but there must have been hope. On this side. The medics applied what was likely an oxygen mask. The eyes were shut. The head lolled with the jolt of the wheels on the sidewalk. If you've ever seen a person near death, you can imagine the marble-like quality the skin takes on.

A sanctified glow.

"Oh, boy," said the big, masked attendant that joined them at the door, in short shirt sleeves, pulling the gurney passed double automated doors. Guiding human traffic. Strange that brief expression we toss about at random as interlude: oh, boy, oh, man... I don't want to say it's like "oh, shit." But I just can't help noticing absence of a second thought.

We don't say, "oh, girl." Not impersonally.

Off-hand.

We got Elizabeth very carefully up to the reception counter. The attendant took our information and pointed to the waiting area. We hovered in the suspension of reality, still slow. Sarah sat patting Elizabeth's hand while gently massaging the area of the back impacted by the thrown rock. My Moms looked small, but calm. Huddled as one.

"I'll get you some water," I said quickly.

The ankle had started to swell. Elizabeth looked up quietly, in restrained pain, giving only a slight nod and appreciative smile.

Walking to the vending machine took me close to the hall where they'd wheeled Evangeline. I was very conscious of near involuntary compulsion to stare. Stare like the rock throwers... I didn't want to, but I went out of my way, looking. I found myself scanning the areas. Loosely curtained compartments back there. Some open, some closed.

And our eyes met.

Unexpectedly. Through a gap. No mask.

The face though vacant was awake. The head, stiffly propped up on the adjustable mattress, looked back at me darkly. The sprawled body was doll size in the high narrow hospital bed.

I noticed that someone had hurriedly hung a hand-written advert in thick black sharpie on the front of the cot rail:

"It. Goes by Zeke."

I could also see that an IV had been inserted into the forearm. Both the wrists were still strapped down. A grudging bit of life was returning, coloring the flesh.... Yellow. The patient was almost indifferent to all the surrounding sounds, lights, and gadgets. I imagined that attendant medics had already administered emergency blood transfusion, the lips still colorless. I wondered if increasing state of "awake" would bring some kind of defined emotion to the eyes. And if so, what. I am afraid to put a question mark on that.

If I had to guess, I'd say anger.

Or disillusionment.

Physical evidence wasn't what bothered. Not as the "look." What I saw. On the outside. No. No, the what bothered was consciousness.

Conscientious choice. What must have occurred sometime prior.

Consciousness chose— chose "It."

And It chose Death.

It's Tabitha that defined it for me.

There are things that are true. Integral. Not put on. You'll notice that for all the things we cloak ourselves with, there are a milliard of things we have not chosen. The things we are given, at birth, and the things that are optional. And our reason, meaning willful choice as acceptance or denial, is where it is all laid bare, like a set of teeth. Either smiling or snarled in defense as if ready to bite.

Remember how I said Tabitha could not hide in a burlap sack? Well, I didn't exactly, but it's that. Not just in sentiment. But internal and external physiology. Strong. What's the word that connotes a lifeforce? Virile. In my eye, the most capable. Of anyone. To give life. It's maybe what makes it all the more tragic, in delivery. I've seen individuals who were broken visibly. By force, or by nature. Being the end of the line.

Preemptively aborting all of mankind.

Like Oli. Like Zeke.

We witnessed this abdication… Tabitha and I. It's like the years go on, and negation is the aftermath. Human mathematics. Multiplication. Division.

Subtraction, following addition. People talk about feminization of boys, the dangers of canned food. An additive in some plastic and metal packaging materials mimicking effects of estrogen. Causing that phenom, the man boob. Nowadays, manufacturers make sure to stick a proud label, "BPA Free."

To help get sales back up.

You would think the feminization of boys would correspond with a masculinization of girls. It didn't. And I can only think one way to phrase the parallel. Seamour never named it.

De-feminization.

My Tabitha looked like a fairytale protagonist. I mean to the very end, Tabitha, I mean Seamour did— I knew they were feeling weak. I can't say how they took the pregnancy. Internally. You know, emotionally. They didn't say. Having beforehand committed to carry. With strength... Quietly... Like an animal that retreats to bear difficult situations alone. Up until the last weeks when premature bleeding made it evident something had gone awry. I want to say circumstantial things...

I recognized our tendency to withdraw, instead of sharing. And I note the parental absence. Of Mother Nature. We're disconnected, not from family. From instinct.

It doesn't exactly "take over."

For so-called survival. Or does it?

I can't help but think of the rest of that Darwin quote: *Every selected character is fully exercised [by Nature], as implied by the fact of their selection.*

Its purpose, whatever it was, fulfilled.

.

I woke up with a start. I sat up in the side chair. I'd been spending vigils in the hospital with short spurts of sleep. The advice had been to allow as much time in the womb. Monitor the bleeding. The precarious positioning requiring carefully controlled delivery.

Not to lose the baby.

Tabitha lay still in the bed.

Sarah had texted.

I answered: *Nine centimeters dilated.*

They think it best to try to wait till contractions start.

I heard a light cough and saw Tabitha's eyes turn on the pillow searching. Searching me out. I saw strained refocusing under lowered eyelashes. The voice a mere wisp when it finally surfaced.

Tabitha said: "We can't keep adding a negative. Eventually we get to zero."

"Less," I said.

If something is missing, or goes missing, it doesn't get filled by taking more and more away. Like sense of self. Recessed.

Each self complementary always to Self.

The silence spoke, loudly in my mind:

I don't want Us to die.

That vacuum. It's an odd thing, a pull. The end.

Tabitha and I suffered from nothing.

It's hard to explain the complete duality. It weighed. We didn't really need for anything. We didn't know lack really. We had all the basics, and then some. Those intangibles that make life extra, like intelligence and talents, good looks. Friendship.

Exceptional attributes, regardless of where they fall on any competitive scale, because of course somebody will always be better than, or equal to, and anyway there is no Math equation.

What is "best?"

Isn't it what we all inherently know?

Singularity.

Uniqueness. Our own.

The isolation of the single sample among other also unique samples, looking out into the world from behind our test slides, for a sliver of similarity among other slides.

When a person wants to kill themselves, I've noticed, it has to do a lot with inertia. The form in which you lose your momentum, and start rolling in reverse. Inwardly. Decision making is stymied. Things happen to you. This pushes you, that hinders you. Outwardly, a horrifying impression of standstill.

The profound burden of *You are doing Nothing*.

Suction. It makes no sense, but no thing bares down more on the conscious mind, than that heft of doing Nothing. Maybe it's the fear that nothing, plus nothing, is more Nothing. And *more nothing* is the only thing worse than Nothing.

That big expanse of empty, useless, already dead space. In reality, Nothing is a beautiful expression.

The Nonexistent, the greatest of all illusions.

Like a single emotion that we would try to name and isolate, out from our constant mixed up chaos. Our quite fertile imagination.

I do recall in oriental tradition it is written: *of all the forms of illusion, woman is the most important.* I pointed that out to Tabitha.

Silence.

"I'm seeing the meaning as the vessel into and out of which other illusions, as lifelines, pour," I said. We were already expecting, I just didn't know it yet. The silence I misunderstood as "skepticism."

But the will to Life is also a kind of suction.

In what it takes. To sustain it. I pulled my hand lightly away from Tabitha's. I was strongly struck in mind and heart: We don't talk enough. No matter how much. Never enough to the ones we would hold closest.

An empty lump gripped my throat from inside.

"Visiting is over," the nurse said, nodding to the patient whose eyes were closed in exhaustion.

Softly, I moved towards the door. The words of the nurse repeated themselves in my ears. It took me a moment to weed through them.

Sounding wrong.

Tabitha was dilated. Labor hadn't started yet. But was eminent. They'd be moving to the delivery area by the patient transport elevator.

To be ready.

And I could follow behind… by *visitor* exit.

"David?"

"Yes," I turned around, caught, like in a movie.

A single highlight catching the eye. Mirrored in mine. A star, that in my focus became as round as the Sun.

"We still have a fighting chance."

I nodded and quietly closed the door.

afterword

If it isn't clear already, this was my person. And I loved this person more than myself.

There I've said it.

I love you.

Ridiculously difficult words to say. And said over and over, can lose something of meaning. That's why these are said sparingly. Reverently. So as not be miscarried.

Like justice.

I was leaving the hospital with a child. This small bundle. A fragment of a father. A fragment of a mother. A complete human. Being.

I want fiercely for this little being to feel complete.

Consequential.

Not saying things doesn't help. Omitting words. Blanking out our physical realities. Censoring self, policing others, in some sort of social politicking.

I could call myself "Parent."

To abstract.

I could wear Tabitha's clothes. Try to claim both. But I would always be Father. As a man.

There was no twisting around that. What sense was there to distance myself from myself, anymore— as They?

Maybe when Seamour died, I lost something of that anonymous detached plurality. That unit of measurement no longer made sense. As needing completion.

Us.

I realized you are as much whole, as part.

I was a piece.

I was one man. Just one man.

And this child's mother was a woman.

One woman.

Tabitha. Seamour... a Rose, if you like.

Not just any woman.

I would be there. You and I had fallen. There was no doubt. From person to person.

All the years we walked, in awe, in wonder, trying
to understand all the world, and each other. Living
and dying—

And I still wanted to catch her.

I felt it like a jolt to the heart the moment the nurse
said, "Congratulations, you have a baby girl."

www.ingramcontent.com/pod-product-compliance
Lightning Source LLC
Chambersburg PA
CBHW020142310726
48970CB00006B/1969